Mills & Boon Classics

A chance to read and collect some of the best-loved novels from Mills & Boon – the world's largest publisher of romantic fiction.

Every month, four titles by favourite Mills & Boon authors will be re-published in the *Classics* series.

A list of other titles in the *Classics* series can be found at the end of this book.

Anne Mather

A SAVAGE BEAUTY

MILLS & BOON LIMITED
LONDON · TORONTO

First published 1973
Australian copyright 1980
Philippine copyright 1980
This edition 1980

© Anne Mather 1973

ISBN 0 263 73277 0

Set in Linotype Plantin 10 on 11½ pt.

*Made and printed in Great Britain by
Richard Clay (The Chaucer Press), Ltd.,
Bungay Suffolk*

CHAPTER ONE

IT was foggy, with one of those fogs that blanketed down suddenly, without warning, and soaked one through with a kind of heavy mist which was much more chilling than actual rain.

It was a night for hugging firesides, thought Emma wearily, pushing her loosened damp hair back from her face for the umpteenth time, and glancing back fearfully along the road behind her as though afraid that something might come hurtling out of the gloom towards her, demolishing her in seconds. She would not have believed she could be within a thirty mile radius of London and yet still find a road which as yet had not a sign of habitation. It was ludicrous really, doubly so when she thought of the annoyance of losing her way in the fog, which, combined with a body-shaking skirmish in a ditch, had left the car temporarily helpless. Added to that she had the ignominy of knowing that she might not easily be able to find the car again, even in daylight, for she hadn't the slightest idea where she was. She had been on the main Guildford to London road, but a roundabout had confused her and when she realized where she was her efforts to turn the car had resulted in her present predicament.

Victor would be furious. He had not wanted her to go to Guildford in the first place, and he had refused to accompany her because he had said she was foolish to go anywhere on such a cold and unpleasant evening. Possibly she had been foolish, she acceded now, but truth to tell, when she had set away from her London home it had only been raining, and no one could have foreseen with any certainty that the evening would turn out the way it had.

But she had gone to Stafford's every year on his birthday,

and as he was her godfather and was in his eighties already, there would not be so many birthdays left for her to visit him. Victor said it was a duty visit, but it wasn't. Stafford Lawson might be old in years, but his mind was as active as ever, and Emma had always enjoyed her visits. It was fortunate, however, that Stafford was also partially blind, or he would never have allowed her to leave after the fog came down.

But Emma had wanted to get home. She had wanted to prove to Victor that she was perfectly capable of driving to Guildford without his escort, in spite of the weather. And now, here she was, lost and alone, without even the benefit of her car. Victor would be bound to find out. Tomorrow he would want to know where her car was and then . . .

She sighed. There was no point in worrying about what Victor might say yet. Her most pressing problem was to find some method of reaching a telephone so that she might summon a taxi and gain the comfort of her father's house in Kensington. What on earth would she do if she didn't come upon some form of habitation soon? And who might she find, she wondered uneasily, out here, miles from anywhere? There were so many stories of young women being lost without trace and her agile mind pondered the possibility of whether any of these disappearances had been in this area.

Angrily, she squashed these ideas. What on earth was she thinking of, allowing her imagination such dramatic rein? In a few minutes she would come upon a cluster of houses or a farm, and when she did so there would be people and lights and telephones, and offers of assistance.

But then another thought struck her. It had been quite late when she left Stafford's, now it must be nearing midnight, and who might be abroad or even awake at such a time? Farmers were early risers, and most probably that was why she had seen no lights. Everyone was in bed!

She shivered. She felt wet and cold and miserable, and this time she was unable to quell the feeling of unease that rose inside her. Whatever was she going to do?

And then, with scarcely a sound except the powerful hiss of heavy tyres on the wet road, she saw a car coming towards her, its yellow fog lamps gradually lifting a little of the gloom around her.

Emma was nonplussed. This was a contingency she had not considered. Who might be driving this car? After her uneasy thoughts of a few moments ago, she was quite prepared to believe that the car's occupant, or occupants, might be wholly undesirable. What ought she to do? What *could* she do? Stop the car and trust that the driver would be an understanding type, or hide until it had passed and hope nobody would notice her white leather coat? Left to herself, she might possibly have decided on the former, but Victor had influenced her life for so long that she automatically turned towards the hedge at the side of the road in an effort to conceal herself because she knew that that was what Victor would have expected her to do. And after all, it was late to expect many decent people to stop.

But although she was wearing boots, their soles were damp and slippery and when they encountered the greasy surface of the turf they caused her to slip and lose her balance. For a moment she remained poised between safety and disaster, desperately trying to right herself, and then, as there was nothing to grab on to and save herself, she fell backwards, awkwardly, into the path of the oncoming automobile.

There was the instant scream of brakes as whoever was driving applied them efficiently, but on the wet road the car still skidded a little before coming to a halt barely inches from Emma herself. Any moment, she expected to feel the crunch of those powerful tyres on her inert body, but the uncanny silence which had fallen following the braking of the car was broken only by the sound of its door opening and being slammed again with obvious impatience. Emma took a shuddering breath. The fall had stunned her, and the realization of how close she had come to death was sufficient to paralyse her. She lay there helplessly, unable to will life into her limbs.

But before she could begin to co-ordinate her thoughts, strong hard hands hauled her unceremoniously to her feet and a stream of harsh vituperative Spanish rang in her ears. Then the man, for no woman could speak so violently, seemed to realize she could not possibly understand and reverting to English, snapped: 'Crazy fool! Throwing yourself into the road like that! Are you in the habit of trying to kill yourself?'

To Emma his anger was the last straw and she felt the hot burning of tears behind her eyes. But she drew herself up to her full height of five feet six inches and faced him bravely. Even so, she had to look up at him, and she blinked rapidly as the dampness misted on her lashes.

'If you think for one moment my action was deliberate then you must be the fool!' she declared fiercely. 'I slipped and I fell!'

The man was looking down at her, but it was too gloomy to distinguish his expression. 'Then please to tell me what you are doing climbing around ditches at this hour of the night on a private road!'

Emma's eyes widened. 'This is a private road? So that explains it!'

'Explains what?' The man was clearly impatient. 'Look, I am getting wet and cold. Where are you bound for? To see Gregory?'

'Gregory?' Emma was vague, and then realizing that this man had no idea of her circumstances, explained: 'No – I was going to London, but I'm afraid I lost my way.' It was no use pretending otherwise. At this hour of the night her

8

motives for being on this man Gregory's private road might be misconstrued unless she was honest.

The man hesitated for a moment and glanced back up the road behind him. 'I see.' He shrugged his shoulders. 'Are you in the habit of walking long distances in such weather?' There was sarcasm in his voice now.

Emma grimaced, and then shivered, and her companion seemed to realize that their conversation could be conducted so much more easily in the warmth of his car.

'Come!' he said. 'I am going to London myself. I will take you there provided you can offer me some reasonable explanation as to why you should be wandering about Paul Gregory's private road at this hour of the night.'

Emma had, perforce, to follow him to his car, but she did so without enthusiasm. Although he had agreed to take her back to town and this knowledge should have filled her with relief, it did not. She had not yet seen his face, she would not have been able to identify him again, and yet she was aware of an air of leashed strength and ruthlessness about him that disturbed her a little. Afterwards she was never quite sure how she had instinctively felt this about him. She only knew that she was reluctant to put herself, however tenuously, into his hands.

The car he was driving, she saw, was a sleek Jensen sports saloon, and inside there was a warm smell of expensive leather and cigars, and what possibly might have been brandy. She glanced across the bonnet at the man as he indicated that she should get into the car and hoped she was not about to make the biggest mistake of her life. What if he had been drinking? She had not smelled alcohol on his breath, but then she had been too disturbed to notice. She sighed, inwardly berating herself. He had stopped expertly enough when she had fallen across his path. That was hardly the reaction of someone who was bemused with drink.

She got slowly into the soft bucket seat and slammed her

door and he did likewise, flicking a switch as he did so which illuminated the interior of the vehicle. Emma blinked again, and put up an involuntary hand to her hair. What a mess she must look, she thought, and knew that had Victor seen her like this he would have been horrified. He was always so conscious of appearances.

Her companion turned to regard her with chilling appraisal, his eyes narrowed, calculating. 'It is interesting to see you in the light, *señorita*,' he observed mockingly, and to her annoyance Emma felt herself colouring, a thing she had not done for years.

But really, he was one of the most disturbing men she had ever encountered. Thick dark hair grew low on his neck, brushing the collar of his dark blue suede jacket in a way which would have caused Victor to twist his lips contemptuously. He abhorred the way men today allowed their hair to grow unchecked, and although he acceded to neatly trimmed sideburns, this was his only concession to modern trends.

This man's sideburns were longer and darkened his already darkly tanned cheekbones, while his eyes were almost black between the longest lashes Emma had ever seen on a man. His features were not regular; his face was thin, his nose decidedly bent, and there were hollows beneath his cheekbones. His mouth was thin, too, and yet it had a sensual curve to it which, added to the arrogant, alien attractiveness of him, caused Emma to feel a disquieting ripple of apprehension along her spine. His intent appraisal was disquieting, too, and as she was unaccustomed to being treated in this way she drummed up a feeling of resentment.

'I can assure you my reasons for being here are entirely respectable,' she said.

His eyes flickered. 'Yes, I am sure they are,' he conceded lazily. 'However, you will forgive me if I choose to make my own assessment of the situation. I should hate to discover to my cost that you were some female decoy waiting to disable me the minute I set the car moving.'

Emma gasped. 'If I were going to do that, I should hardly wait until the car was moving, would I? Whatever would I do with you slumped over the wheel?'

'A pleasant thought,' he agreed, with a wry twist to his mouth, and Emma looked abruptly away. She couldn't encounter that lazy mocking gaze of his, and in any case, the way he looked at her made her feel uncomfortable. He was obviously used to dealing with members of her sex, and from his attitude she guessed he was probably aware of his own attractions. He was young, too, only about thirty or thirty-two, and although she knew she had never met him before, there was something vaguely familiar about him. She quelled her curiosity. This would never do. So long as he sat there looking at her, making her aware of every inch of her own body, they would not get back to London.

As though realizing her discomfort, he raised his hand and flicked out the light, leaning forward to start the powerful engine. 'Very well,' he said, as the car's wheels began to roll forward, 'now tell me: why are you wandering about in the fog? He glanced her way speculatively. 'Trouble with a man, perhaps?'

Emma, who had been relaxing, stiffened. 'Of course not,' she denied sharply.

'Why – of course not? It's a reasonable supposition. From the look of you, I'd say you'd been grappling with more than just the weather!'

Emma moved awkwardly, putting up a hand to her hair. Of course, she must look a mess. Her hair, which had begun the evening in its usual sleek pleat, hung in untidy strands down her back, while her face was devoid of all make-up.

'I went to see a friend in Guildford,' she explained in

controlled tones. 'But coming back I lost my way in the fog, and when I discovered I was on the wrong road and tried to turn the car, it ended up in a ditch.'

'Another ditch?' There was a trace of amusement in his voice.

'Yes, another ditch,' she answered abruptly.

'And you came all the way from London in these conditions to see this friend? A man, without a doubt, señorita.'

'Not in the way you mean,' retorted Emma annoyedly.

'What way do I mean?' he inquired innocently, and Emma had to bite her lips to prevent herself from making some angry reply. He was deliberately baiting her, amusing himself at her expense, and while he was obviously used to this kind of verbal thrust and parrying, she was not. Victor didn't go in for playing with words.

'I don't think my reasons for going to Guildford are any concern of yours,' she stated coldly. 'I shall be very grateful if you could simply take me to the nearest taxi rank. I can easily get a cab.'

'Don't be so quick to take offence, señorita,' he advised her dryly. 'For someone who until a few minutes ago was lost, cold and bedraggled, you show a definite lack of appreciation.'

Emma felt a sense of contrition at this words. She was indebted to him, and she was allowing his attitude to influence hers. Endeavouring to speak naturally, she said: 'I'm sorry. I know I must sound ungrateful, but I'm not really. It's simply that I'm not used to coping with this kind of a situation.' She made a deprecatory movement towards her hair. 'I must look a terrible mess!'

He glanced briefly in her direction and then returned his attention to the shrouded road ahead. 'I shouldn't alarm yourself. A beautiful woman usually manages to look good whatever the circumstances.'

Emma caught her breath. 'Beautiful?' she echoed, her lips moving uncertainly. And then the colour in her cheeks deepened as she thought she saw a faint twisted smile on his lips. 'You're very polite!' There was sarcasm in her voice now.

'Polite? Why should you think that? You are beautiful, and I'm quite sure you're aware of the fact, so why deny it?'

Emma gasped. 'No one has ever described me that way before,' she asserted dryly.

'No? Well, I've always thought Englishmen lacked perception.' His long fingers slid expertly round the steering wheel. 'Among other things,' he added mockingly.

Emma forced herself to take note of her surroundings. For the last few moments she had been so intent on what her companion had been saying that she had half forgotten her reasons for being in his car in the first place.

Amber lights burning ahead of them signified the roundabout on the main Guildford to London road and she sighed with relief. At last she knew where she was again.

She paused to wonder whether if she contacted a garage in the morning they would send someone out to locate her car. No doubt if Victor contacted them it would carry more weight, but she was not looking forward to explaining the details of her homeward journey to him, particularly after he had advised her not to go. She sighed. If she had heeded his advice she would not now be installed in this sleek, luxurious automobile with a man who, apart from his obvious material attributes, possessed a strong sexual attraction that disturbed Emma's normally placid disposition. Her eyes drifted continually in his direction, to that lean dark profile, sliding over the soft expensive suede of his suit to the strong hands gripping the wheel.

A moment later he startled her by leaning forward, flicking open the glove compartment and extracting a slim

13

gold case. 'Cigarette?' he offered.

Emma swallowed quickly. 'I – I'm trying to give them up,' she answered automatically. It was true; Victor had been trying to persuade her to do so for weeks. But even as she said the words she wished she could retract them. Right now, a cigarette was what she needed to calm her nerves.

The man shrugged, dropping the case on to the parcel shelf, and drew a narrow cigar out of his pocket, putting it between his lips and flicking a lighter. The exhalation of smoke was intoxicating to Emma. She sighed, almost unconsciously, and he glanced at her again.

'You want a cigarette? Have one. They're not marijuana.'

'I never thought they were,' she exclaimed indignantly.

'But I am right, aren't I? You would like a cigarette.'

She bent her head. 'Yes.'

'Then have one, for God's sake!' He leant forward and lifting the slim gold case dropped it into her lap. 'Here. Help yourself.'

Emma opened the case and put one of the long American cigarettes between her lips. But when she would have searched in her handbag for a light he flicked the lighter he had used and she leant forward to apply the tip of her cigarette to the flame. She steadied his hand with hers, conscious of his hard skin beneath her fingers. She was conscious of him, too, and she was almost sure he knew it. She drew back abruptly when her cigarette was lit, breathing deeply.

'Is it good?' he asked, and she nodded.

'Marvellous! I needed it.'

He drew on his own cigar and concentrated on the lights of a solitary vehicle ahead of them and Emma relaxed a little. They would be approaching the outskirts of the city soon and then it would not be long before she was home. If Mrs. Cook was still up she would be worried about her. Emma only hoped the housekeeper had not had the idea of phoning Victor when she was so late. While her father was away Mrs. Cook felt a strong sense of responsibility for Emma.

As they neared the suburbs, traffic became a little more frequent even though it was so late, and there were one or two people making their way home from parties and such like. They crossed Putney Bridge, but when they stopped at some traffic lights, Emma said:

'I can take a cab from here.'

The lights changed and the powerful Jensen rolled forward without letting her out. 'If you tell me where you live, I'll drive you home. But you will have to direct me. My knowledge of London is limited to its main thoroughfares.'

'That's not necessary, thank you,' replied Emma quickly. 'I wouldn't dream of taking you out of your way.'

The street lights were casting some illumination into the car now and she could see the faint mockery about his mouth. 'You are perhaps afraid your husband may see us together?'

Emma's eyes widened. 'Of course not.'

'There is no husband?' He frowned.

'No.' She felt herself colouring again.

'*Hombre!* I am surprised. Are not most English girls of your age married?'

Emma resented his tone of voice. 'I am twenty-five, *señor*, that's all. Why should you imagine I should necessarily be married?'

He raised dark eyebrows. 'In my country, it is much different. At eighteen a girl is already a wife and mother.'

Emma speculated what country that might be. Although he was obviously Spanish, or at least of Spanish descent, she somehow doubted he came from Spain itself. There was a vaguely American inflection in his English and she thought he might come from one of the South American republics.

'Strange as it may seem, *señor*, I have no particular desire to become a mother yet.'

His eyes narrowed. 'I notice you do not say – a *wife* and mother. I take it the one is more desirable to you than the other.'

Emma felt impatient. 'If you insist on taking me home, *señor*, I live in Kensington. We turn left at the next junction.'

It was comparatively easy to reach Emma's father's house in Dudley Gardens from Warwick Road, and as the fog was so much less dense here she knew he would have no difficulty in finding his way back to the main road again. When the car halted smoothly at the gates to the short drive, Emma turned to him politely.

'Thank you very much,' she said, hoping she sounded less nervous than she felt. 'I don't know how I should have got home without your assistance.'

He shrugged his broad shoulders lazily. 'No doubt you would have reached Paul Gregory's house eventually,' he remarked. 'You were going in the right direction and one way or another you'd have been able to make some arrangement there, I'm sure.'

'Nevertheless, you've been very kind.' Emma fumbled for the door catch without success, and without a word he leant past her and thrust open the door. For a brief moment, his hard arm was against her breasts, and she smelt the faint masculine aroma of his skin, and then she was tumbling out of the car, almost tripping in her haste. As she turned to close the door, the interior light was on and she encountered his dark disturbing gaze.

'Good – good night,' she said unevenly.

'*Adios!*' He smiled faintly, and then as the door slammed and the light went out, he drove swiftly away. And as he went Emma felt again that disturbingly positive notion that she had seen him before. But how was that possible? He was certainly not Victor's type, nor was he likely to move in Victor's circle. No. It was probably that he reminded her of someone, but who?

With a sigh, she turned and went slowly up the drive to the front door. As she did so, the hall light came on and the door opened to reveal Mrs. Cook, the housekeeper, wrapped in a warm red woollen dressing gown.

'Miss Emma!' she exclaimed, with relief. 'Thank heavens you're back. It's after one o'clock. I've been so worried about you. I was just about to ring Mr. Harrison and ask his advice when I heard the car.'

Emma stepped into the hall, loosening the white leather coat automatically, and as she did so Mrs. Cook gave another exclamation. 'Is something wrong, miss? Your hair – I mean – you look so dishevelled. Has there been an accident?'

Emma shook her head, throwing her coat on to the chest in the carpeted hallway. 'Not exactly, Mrs. Cook,' she answered carefully. 'And I'm glad you didn't ring Mr. Harrison. I shouldn't like to worry him unnecessarily.' She walked down the hall and into the comfortable living-room, appreciating the warmth generated from the radiators. 'What a terrible night!'

Mrs. Cook clicked her tongue with the familiarity of long service. 'Where have you been, Miss Emma?' she asked reprovingly. 'And why did you come home in another car? Where's the Mini?'

'All in good time, Mrs. Cook.' Emma ran a hand over her tumbled hair. 'Tell me, is there any coffee on the stove?'

'At this time of night?' Mrs. Cook looked scandalized. Then she sighed. 'Oh, well, yes, I suppose I can get you some.'

Emma followed the housekeeper into the large modern kitchen at the back of the house, and perched on a stool at the breakfast bar while Mrs. Cook plugged in the percolator and set it bubbling.

'Now,' she said, when that was done, 'what happened?'

'I ditched the car in the fog,' said Emma bluntly. 'I had to hitch a ride home.'

'What?' Mrs. Cook was horrified.

'It's true. I lost my way. Then when I tried to turn the car I ran into a ditch. I couldn't get it out again.'

Mrs. Cook wrapped her dressing gown closer about her. 'It's just as well your father's not here,' she stated rebukingly. 'Can you imagine how worried he would have been?' Then she frowned. 'And who was it who gave you a lift?'

'I don't know.' Emma shrugged. 'I didn't ask his name, and he didn't ask mine.'

'I see.' Mrs. Cook turned back to attend to the coffee. 'Well, it seems to me you've been remarkably lucky getting a lift at this time of night. Where's your car now?'

'I don't know.' Emma made a helpless gesture as Mrs. Cook began to look impatient again. 'Well, I don't. Somewhere off the Guildford road, I guess. I should think if I give some details to an agency, they'll find it for me and bring it back. I just don't want Victor to know, that's all.'

'Mr. Harrison is bound to find out,' said Mrs. Cook disapprovingly.

'Why should he? Unless you tell him, of course.'

Mrs. Cook shook her head, pushing a mug of creamy coffee towards her. 'These things have a habit of coming out, given time,' she replied dampeningly.

'Not necessarily,' retorted Emma, lifting the cup and scenting the aroma experimentally. 'Hmm, this is good. Thank you. You're a darling!'

Mrs. Cook sniffed. 'And you're spoiled, that's the trouble with you,' she asserted, but there was an unwilling twinkle in her eyes. 'And I'm away to my bed now, if you've everything you need. I have to get up in the morning.'

Emma wrinkled her nose. 'All right, Mrs. Cook. And

thanks again.'

Later, in her own room, Emma viewed her appearance without pleasure. She was horrified to discover that her nose was smudged with soot, and that her hair tumbled loosely almost to her waist. She extracted the few remaining hairpins and ran a brush through its tangled length. Loosened, it was the colour of burnt amber, thick and silky, glowing with health. But she invariably wore it in either a pleat or a chignon, and its colour was then subdued to a dark auburn. Victor preferred it confined. He didn't like loose hair. Maybe he considered it made her look rather young and unsophisticated. He could be sensitive about things like that.

Cupping her chin in her hands, she stared into the wide-spaced grey eyes which were reflected in the mirror. Without make-up her skin was creamy smooth, her lashes dark and thick, shadowing her cheeks. A tissue removed the smudges of soot from her nose and she regarded herself critically. Her hair did look more feminine loose like this, but a gust of wind would send it into wild disorder and Victor hated to find hairs on his immaculately tailored jackets. Her make-up was always very correct, foundation, powder and a bright but not vivid lipstick, and yet she was realizing now that without any colour added to her lips they looked fuller and more sensual . . .

She rose angrily to her feet. Whatever was she thinking of? What was the matter with her, sitting here assessing her potentialities? She was not a teenager, she was a mature woman of twenty-five, a woman moreover who was engaged to be married to a man quite a lot of years older than herself who was entirely satisfied with her the way she was. Why was she considering ways of improving her appearance? It was ridiculous, ludicrous, pathetic!

She began to take off her clothes quickly, but before going into the bathroom for her shower she glimpsed her naked body in the mirror and hesitated again. Her limbs were long and slender, her hips firm and curving, her breasts warmly rounded; was she a fool not to exploit her body more, to make herself attractive to other men as well as to Victor?

With determined steps she marched into the bathroom. Hell, she thought irritatedly, just because some man, some stranger, had suggested that it was high time she was married, she was allowing his uncultivated beliefs to intrude upon hers. She had not wanted to get married; she had been perfectly happy looking after her father until Victor came along. Why should she feel guilty because of that?

She drew off her diamond engagement ring and regarded it intently for a few minutes before turning on the shower. In any case, she told herself grimly, inadvertently stepping under the shower without her cap and soaking her loosened hair so that it clung in curling tendrils about her back and shoulders, the man she had encountered this evening was not at all the sort of person Victor would want her to associate with. Victor was not narrow-minded, he liked her to have friends of her own, and she did, but somehow she sensed that the dark stranger of the fog would not fall into that category.

CHAPTER TWO

THE next morning Emma slept late and she was awakened by the sound of raised voices in the hall downstairs. For several minutes she lay there listening, wondering if Mrs. Cook was having an altercation with the butcher, but then she realized it was Victor's voice.

Leaning over, she examined the clock on her bedside table, focusing on it with difficulty. It was after eleven-thirty, and she scrambled hastily out of bed, pulling on a soft brushed nylon housecoat over her nightdress, wondering apprehensively what Victor was doing here at this hour and what, if anything, Mrs. Cook had told him about the night before.

As she opened her bedroom door, she could hear Victor saying impatiently: 'But what time will she be up? I can't hang about here all day. I have work to do.'

Emma went to the head of the stairs. 'Victor!' she exclaimed, beginning to descend slowly. 'I didn't know you were coming this morning. I'm sorry I wasn't up when you arrived. I'm afraid I've overslept.'

Victor Harrison regarded her with disapproval, and Emma became self-consciously aware of her state of *déshabille*. Beside his sleek business suit she felt hopelessly out of place, and a feeling of embarrassment swept over her. But Victor always looked immaculate and as he was a tall, broad man, his clothes fitted him with elegance. Although he was in his late forties, and his hair was tinged with grey in places, he had a very distinguished appearance, and Emma had always admired him. His waistline was thickening now with so many business lunches to attend, but his height could stand it without it becoming too noticeable.

When they went out together Emma always tried to emulate his elegant example.

But this morning the contrast between them was strongly marked, and Emma wished she had stopped and brushed her hair and put on some clothes before coming downstairs.

'I came to see whether you'd like to have lunch with me,' Victor said now, casting a dismissing glance in Mrs. Cook's direction. The housekeeper tactfully murmured something about coffee and disappeared into the kitchen, and sighing, Emma said: 'Come into the lounge, Victor. We can't talk here.'

She led the way into a high-ceilinged room to the right of the hall where a warm fire burned in the grate. The flames reflected in the rosewood of the baby grand that stood in one corner, and cast shadows on the pale walls. Although the house was centrally heated, Emma's father insisted on keeping a fire in this room. It had been her mother's domain and Emma found the cheerful glow comforting as well as warming.

Victor followed her reluctantly, and she gave him an appealing smile. 'I'm sorry, darling. I don't normally appear like this at lunchtime.'

'I should hope not.' Victor sighed, running a hand over his hair. 'Did you get to Guildford last evening?'

Emma turned away so that he could not see her face, nodding. 'Yes. Stafford was delighted to see me. I was glad I took the trouble.'

Victor accepted this without comment. It was obvious he did not connect the fact of her oversleeping with her visit to Guildford.

'And how long will it take you – to – well – make yourself presentable?' Victor was asking now, and she swung round frowning.

'You'll wait?'

'I shall have to, shan't I?' Victor looked irritable.

'Where are we lunching?'

'The Dorchester.' Victor thrust his hands into the pockets of his trousers. 'Sir Malcolm wants to discuss the Messiter deal with me and this is his only opportunity. But as his daughter's in London at the moment, he suggested we make up a foursome for lunch.'

'Oh, I see. A business lunch.' Emma was less than enthusiastic. 'Do I have to attend?'

Victor's square face became stiff. 'You don't *have* to do anything, of course. I simply thought that as my fiancée you'd want to take an interest in my affairs.'

'But, darling, your business affairs have nothing to do with me.'

'On the contrary, they have everything to do with you. Once Messiter Textiles comes within the sphere of Harrison Interloop, we shall hold a tremendous influence—'

'All right, all right,' Emma interrupted him with a sigh. She had no intention of allowing Victor to go into a long monologue about the possibilities of cornering the textile market. 'I'll come. Mrs. Cook is making some coffee, so you help yourself and I'll go and take a shower.'

'Very well.' Victor's face relaxed agreeably, and Emma waited for a few moments to see whether he would now relax sufficiently to kiss her, to show her in some way that he was glad to see her. But Victor merely smiled in a satisfied way and took up a position in front of the fire, obviously prepared to wait for her to go and get ready. With an impatient gesture Emma left the room and encountered Mrs. Cook in the hall, on her way to the lounge with a tray of coffee.

'Well?' said the housekeeper, looking knowingly at Emma's exasperated expression. 'Are you lunching out?'

'Oh, yes. Yes, of course.' Emma brushed past her and ran up the stairs to her room, but once there she flung off her clothes irritably. Couldn't Victor sometimes let himself go and show a little emotion? Heavens, it wasn't as though he had never seen a woman in a dressing gown before; he had been married for almost fifteen years. Surely in that time he had grown used to seeing a woman about his home. He must have become accustomed to his wife, invalid though she had been; used to entering her bedroom, sleeping in her bed!

Emma went into her bathroom with ill-concealed dissatisfaction. Although she had known him for five years, although they had been engaged for almost six months, they had never got beyond the stage of gentle lovemaking he had first courted her with. And although it was rare that Emma ever felt that their relationship was not developing in the way that it should, today she felt inordinately dissatisfied with her lot. She wished her father would come back. Perhaps it was being alone so much that was unsettling her.

But then she heaved a sigh. Her father was enjoying himself in Canada with her older brother and his wife, and as he had now retired from medical practice, there was nothing to stop him from remaining there another three months. He knew Emma was well looked after by Mrs. Cook, and in any case he considered her a sensible girl.

During the following week, life settled back into its normal pattern. Emma worked part-time for a friend in a secretarial agency off Oxford Street, more for something to do than for the money involved, for although she had been offered a place at university seven years ago her mother had died at that time and she had known that as her brother was already married she could not leave home and her father alone. In consequence, she took a secretarial course at a London technical college and eventually joined Fenella Harding at the agency.

Fenella was older than Emma, a contemporary of Victor's, in fact, and it had been through Fenella that Emma had first met her fiancé. Even so, the idea that the big, powerful industrialist should take anything more than a fleeting interest in her had never occurred to her until he introduced himself to Dr. Seaton and slowly but surely eased himself into her life. Emma had always been rather shy and withdrawn, preferring the company of books to that of the opposite sex, and Victor's worldly manner had aroused a sense of admiration in her. That he was so much older than she was had been unimportant. She had never considered herself a particularly trendy sort of person. Her clothes were square, the other girls in the office said so, and since she had taken to wearing her hair in its pleat, she knew she looked years older.

But Victor approved, and after all, that was all that really mattered.

The afternoon following her unfortunate accident in the fog, she had managed to contact a garage in the Guildford area who, for a fee, had been prepared to locate the whereabouts of her car from the description of the circumstances she was able to give them. The Mini had been returned to her as good as new, and Victor had learned nothing of the incident, much to her relief.

All the same, from time to time, she couldn't help pondering the identity of the man who had rescued her and brought her home. The certainty that she had seen him before had strengthened and it was a tantalizing puzzle which intrigued her. But as such thoughts were abortive she endeavoured to put all such speculation to the back of her mind.

On Friday evening it was late when Emma left the agency. They had had rather a panic on that afternoon, as several of the girls were away with 'flu, and consequently they were inundated with work. Emma had volunteered to stay on as Victor was away in Brighton for the evening, attending a business dinner, and she did not expect to see him again until the following afternoon.

It was a cold, frosty evening when she emerged from the office building, but there was no fog, and she breathed deeply, enjoying the feeling of release. She walked the few yards to where the Mini was parked and drove home without incident, parking it in the drive before entering the house.

'Mrs. Cook!' she called. 'I'm home!'

There was no immediate response and, shrugging, Emma crossed the hall to the lounge, unbuttoning her tweed overcoat, thrusting open the door to enter the comfortable lamp-lit room. As she did so, a man rose from his position on the couch, and she stepped back in alarm, a hand pressed to her lips. But as the man moved into the light, she said incredulously: '*You!* What are you doing here?'

The dark Spanish-American regarded her intently. 'I came to see you,' he replied simply, but his eyes were surveying her with a mixture of doubt and disbelief.

Emma put up a hand to her hair. It was as smooth and elegant as ever, her blue tweed suit beneath the matching coat beautifully tailored, but rather severe in style. She was conscious of feeling years older than he was as he stood there so dark and lean and attractive in a close-fitting cream suede suit that moulded every muscle of his thighs.

'I – well – have you been waiting long?' she asked nervously, unable to assimilate the situation with any degree of composure. 'Did Mrs. Cook let you in?'

'Your housekeeper?' He raised his dark eyebrows. 'Yes, she let me in. She didn't want to, but when I explained who I was . . .' His voice trailed away. 'You've suffered no ill effects of your midnight ramblings, I see.'

'Oh, no – no!' Emma glanced over her shoulder uneasily. 'I – I'm very grateful to you for helping me.'

The man inclined his head politely and she rubbed her finger tips together rather awkwardly. Why had he come? Had she left something in his car? But no, if she had, she would have missed whatever it was by now, wouldn't she?

Her eyes alighted on the drinks cabinet in the corner. 'Er – did Mrs. Cook – that is – can I offer you a drink?' she inquired, stepping forward again.

'Thank you,' he nodded, and she walked jerkily across the room to the cabinet, conscious of his eyes upon her the whole time.

'Wh-what would you like?' she asked, inspecting the bottles. 'Scotch? Gin? Brandy?'

'Scotch would be fine,' he replied calmly, folding his hands behind his back. His jacket was unfastened and the lapels parted to reveal a dark blue shirt and matching tie beneath. Emma's eyes were drawn to him almost against her will, and she had to force herself to concentrate on what she was doing.

As it was the bottle jangled noisily against the glass, and he moved swiftly across to her with lithe grace and took it from her unresisting fingers. 'I'll do it,' he said, and she stood aside and let him. The Scotch poured smoothly into the glass, the bottle was put back in its place, and he raised the Scotch to his lips. '*Salud!*' he said, and swallowed half of it at a gulp.

Emma moved uncomfortably. She was suddenly aware of the quiet intimacy of the room, of his nearness, and of the fact that were Victor to come upon them suddenly he could only assume the worst.

'Won't you join me?' he was asking now, but Emma shook her head.

'No, thank you.' She moved away from him nervously, and with a careless shrug he lifted his glass and emptied it. She was aware that his eyes never left her. They moved over her insolently, intently, assessing her; and it was a disturbing experience for someone who was not used to this kind of mental assault.

As though sensing her unease he moved, his eyes drifting

round the attractively appointed room. The wide couch of soft tan leather was complemented by the dull green velvet of the long curtains, while the carpet underfoot was a mixture of autumn shades.

But his eyes lingered longest on the piano, and without asking permission, he walked across to the instrument, sitting down on the matching stool and running his long brown fingers lightly over the keys.

And then she saw who he was, and the sudden realization caused her to utter a faint gasp. He was Miguel Salvaje. And that was why she had thought his face was familiar. She had seen a picture of him in a newspaper only a few weeks ago when his arrival in this country from Mexico had been widely reported in the press.

He looked up at her exclamation and the long black lashes veiled his eyes. 'Well, Miss Seaton?' he challenged softly.

Emma's lips parted involuntarily. 'You know my name!'

He inclined his head slowly. 'And you know mine, do you not?'

Emma nodded. 'I'm sorry. I should have recognized you sooner.'

'Why?' His eyes narrowed. 'Are you a lover of classical music, Miss Seaton?'

Emma shrugged awkwardly. 'I like all kinds of music,' she said. 'I – I've never attended one of your concerts, but I do have some of your records. My – my mother was a keen pianist herself.'

'And you?'

'Oh, no.' Emma shook her head. 'Just to fifth grade. I'm afraid I'm not a very artistic person, *señor*.' She frowned. 'But how do you know my name?'

He rose from the piano stool and came towards her until they were only about a foot apart. 'I was curious about you,' he replied. 'I wanted to see you again.'

Emma felt herself colouring. She couldn't help it. He was so direct. And how could she answer that?

But in fact she didn't have to. Instead, he went on: 'Tell me! Now that we have been more or less introduced, why do you wear these clothes? Are they – how do you say it – your working clothes?'

Emma was taken aback. 'I – I don't know what you mean.'

'Of course you do.' His dark eyes were disturbingly tense. 'I do not like them. Take them off!'

Emma was horrified. 'What did you say?'

'I asked you to take off these – garments,' he returned smoothly. 'Go! Change! I will wait for you.'

Emma was astounded. 'Señor Salvaje, I don't know what customs you have in your country, but in England one cannot simply walk into a person's house and demand that they change their clothes for your benefit,' she declared heatedly.

Miguel half smiled. 'No?'

'No.' Emma took a deep breath, conscious of a sense of breathlessness that no amount of deep breathing would assuage. 'Look, *señor*, I don't know why you came here, but—'

'I told you. I came to see you,' he interrupted her softly.

Emma's palms moistened. 'I – this is ridiculous! You really must excuse me, *señor*. I – er – Mrs. Cook will be wondering where I am – whether I'm ready for dinner—'

'You are running away from me, Emma. Why?'

The way he said her name with its foreign inflection was a caress and Emma's heart pounded furiously. 'Please, *señor*—' she began, but he shook his head.

'Invite me to dinner,' he suggested. 'I am a stranger, away from my own country. Surely you would not refuse a stranger a meal?'

Emma stared at him helplessly. Then she tugged off her overcoat. Her body was overheated already, and the atmosphere in the room was electric. 'I would like you to go, *señor*,' she said carefully. 'I – I'm very tired.'

'So am I,' he remarked lazily. 'There have been concerts every night this week. This is my first free evening.'

Emma made an impotent gesture. 'I don't understand you.'

'No. I would agree with you there,' he conceded, unbuttoning the top two buttons of his shirt and pulling down his tie so that she could see the brown column of his throat. His skin was deeply tanned and for a brief moment she recalled Victor's pale flesh, sallow from too many hours spent in boardrooms, loose from lack of exercise. Miguel Salvaje did not appear to have an ounce of spare flesh on his body, and the muscles of his chest rippled beneath the dark blue silk of his shirt as he moved. Emma was self-consciously aware of noticing this, and guiltily forced her eyes away from him. In a tight little voice, she said:

'Will you please leave, *señor*?'

Miguel made an impatient gesture. 'And if I choose not to do so? What then? What will you do? Will you call the *policia*? Will you have me humiliated in the eyes of the public – of the press?'

Emma doubted that anyone or anything could humiliate him. Indeed, the humiliation would be all hers. Making a last desperate attempt to appeal to him, she exclaimed: 'Are you so desperate for companionship, *señor*, that you would spend an evening with someone who does not want your company?'

He uttered an imprecation. 'Yes,' he replied harshly. 'Yes, I need companionship. I want to relax away from my work – away from the things that bring it constantly to mind. You do not wish me to dine here with you – very well, I accept that. Then let me buy you dinner somewhere. Surely there

30

are restaurants where we need not be formal, where no one will recognize me!'

Emma moved uncomfortably towards the door. 'I'm afraid that's out of the question, *señor*.'

'Why? Why is it out of the question? I would like to spend an evening with you, and I think you would not find it so objectionable, in spite of what you say.'

Indignation flooded her at his words. Did he imagine her refusal was merely a coy attempt to increase his interest? And to suggest that she would be prepared to eat with him at some out-of-the-way restaurant so that none of his friends or associates should learn of their association was insulting. What had she done to make him think she would welcome his attentions? Did he assume that as she was a woman who on his own admission he considered to be past marriageable age she would welcome an affair with someone like himself? How dared he? The audacity of it all!

Her breasts rose and fell with the tumult of her emotions, and she found it difficult to articulate clearly. 'I – I can assure you, *señor*, that *I* am not desperate for company. And if my fiancé were here you would not dare to speak to me in this way—'

'Fiancé?' His thin face was sardonic. 'You have a fiancé, *señorita*?' He shrugged. 'A *novio*? I am not interested in your *novio*.'

Emma gave an exasperated ejaculation. 'What does it take to convince you that I mean what I say?' she demanded. 'Is this the way you treat women in your country, *señor*?'

He shook his head slowly. 'In my country? No. But this is not my country.'

Emma sighed. Where was Mrs. Cook? Why didn't she come? Surely she must have heard her come in, must know she would be shocked to find this man waiting for her.

Miguel Salvaje continued to regard her for a few moments longer and then his lean fingers slid up and tightened his tie again. She noticed inconsequently that he wore a ring on his left hand, a carved antique gold ring that made a fitting setting for a ruby that glowed with an inner fire all its own.

He inclined his head. 'It shall be as you insist, *señorita*. I regret the intrusion.'

He walked towards the door, and as he did so Emma felt a terrible sense of compunction. But why should she? she asked herself impatiently. Just because for a brief moment he had seemed completely defenceless she should not fool herself into thinking it was anything more than another attempt to get her to change her mind. She must remember he was Miguel Salvaje, rich, clever, aware of his own potentialities, prepared to use her as no doubt he had used other women in other cities, and not merely a lonely man seeking companionship.

She sighed, but he did not look back and a few moments later she heard the sound of the outer door closing. He had gone. She hesitated only a moment, and then she rushed across to the window, drawing aside the curtain and peering out. He was walking down the short drive, his shoulders hunched, his hands thrust into the pockets of his jacket. He didn't have an overcoat and she thought he must be frozen, used as he was to a warmer climate in any case. Where was his car? She frowned. She didn't remember seeing it as she came in. Surely she would have noticed such a conspicuous automobile if it had been parked anywhere near the house.

She bit her lip hard, but he had disappeared into the street and the hedges of the house next door hid him from sight. She allowed the curtain to fall back into place and as she did so Mrs. Cook came into the room.

'Oh, you're home, Miss Emma!' she exclaimed. 'I didn't hear you come in. When I heard the door just now—' She looked round. 'Has Señor Salvaje left?'

Emma cupped the back of her neck with her hands. 'It looks like it, doesn't it?' she asked impatiently. 'You knew who he was, then?'

'Of course.'

'I didn't know you were interested in music, Mrs. Cook.'

'Interested in music?' Mrs. Cook frowned. 'What do you mean?'

Emma stared at her. 'I thought you said you knew who he was.'

'Yes. He introduced himself to me. I understood he was the gentleman who brought you home the other evening.'

'He was – he *is*!' Emma heaved a deep breath. 'He's also a concert pianist.'

'Is he?' Mrs. Cook made a suitably respectful grimace. 'I didn't know that. Anyway, what did he want?'

Emma shrugged. 'I don't really know. He – well, he invited me to have dinner with him.'

Mrs. Cook raised her eyebrows. 'Indeed? And what would Mr. Harrison say to that, I wonder?'

'Well, you've no need to, Mrs. Cook. Because I'm not going.'

Mrs. Cook nodded slowly. 'Well, I just came to see what time you wanted your meal. Are you ready now?'

Emma looked down at the severe lines of her suit irritably. Then she shook her head. 'No, not yet. I want to change first.'

'Change?' Mrs. Cook couldn't hide her curiosity. 'Are you going out again then?'

Emma shook her head. 'No – no, I'm not going out again, Mrs. Cook. I merely want to change, that's all.' Her tone was eloquent of her resentment at Mrs. Cook's probing.

'Yes, miss!' Mrs. Cook was offended, her back stiff and unyielding as she went out again. Emma kicked off her shoes ill-temperedly. What was the matter with her? Speaking to

Mrs. Cook like that! There was no cause for it.

Clenching her teeth, she marched out of the room and up the stairs. It was as though contact with that man, Miguel Salvaje, disrupted her. The last time she had felt like this was when he had brought her home in the fog, and now here she was a mass of conflicting emotions, just because he had taken it upon himself to enter her life again. It was stupid and childish. She wasn't an adolescent, so why was she behaving like one?

All the same, she found herself thinking about him a lot through that long evening, wondering where he was and what he was doing, and whether he had found someone else to keep him company . . .

CHAPTER THREE

DURING the following week, Emma endeavoured to put all thoughts of Miguel Salvaje out of her mind. But that was easier said than done. She had only to open a newspaper it seemed to see his face staring back at her, or some other advertisement of the fact that the Mexican pianist was presently giving a series of recitals with the accompaniment of the London Symphony Orchestra at the Festival Hall.

For the first time in her life she wished she had a close girl friend, someone of her own age in whom she might confide her fears and anxieties. But the girl she had been closest to had married some years ago and gone to live in the Midlands, and now there was only Victor, and of course she could say nothing to him. So she kept her thoughts to herself and concentrated her energies on her work at the agency.

Nevertheless, she was still taken aback when one afternoon her fiancé walked into the agency and after a casual word with Fenella came over to her desk. Perching himself on the side of the desk, he looked down into her face and said, without warning: 'Miguel Salvaje is a favourite of yours, isn't he?'

Emma's hands trembled and she thrust them on to her lap so that he should not see them, but she could not prevent the colour from leaving her cheeks. 'Wh – what did you say?' she asked weakly.

'Miguel Salvaje. You like his playing, don't you?'

Emma tried to gather her scattered composure. 'I – I – yes, I suppose so. Why – why?'

Victor shrugged his broad shoulders. 'I've got these.' He put his hand into his inside pocket and drew out two tickets. 'They're complimentary. You know the sort of thing they distribute to firms. Well, these came into my hands, and I thought we might go. But as they're for this evening, I thought I had better give you warning.'

Emma swallowed convulsively. The very last thing she wanted was to attend one of Miguel's concerts. She didn't want to see him again, to feel that awful, irritable, unsettled feeling he generated inside her.

'Oh, I don't know, Victor,' she temporized awkwardly. 'I – we're awfully busy here at the agency. I don't know if I'll be able to get away in time . . .'

Victor frowned, and then swung round to face Fenella Harding. 'Hey, Fenella,' he said. 'There's no reason why Emma should work late this evening, is there?'

Fenella looked surprised. 'Of course not.' Her delicately plucked brows drew together. 'Did you say there was, Emma?'

Emma shook her head. 'Not exactly.'

Victor turned back to her. 'Don't you want to go or something? I thought you liked Salvaje! You have his records.'

'I know I do.' Emma felt desperate. What could she say? How could she convince him she didn't want to go without arousing his suspicions? Victor could be a very possessive man. 'It's just such short notice, Victor.'

'Oh, come on. It's not a première I'm taking you to. It's a concert. Go home, get changed, and I'll pick you up about seven. We'll have a drink beforehand and supper afterwards, right?'

'All right.' Emma nodded and shrugging again Victor slid off the desk.

'Must go. Got an appointment in half an hour. See you later, then, my dear.'

'Yes.'

Emma watched him go through the door, tall and immaculate in his city clothes. Then she looked down mutinously at her typewriter. She had not wanted to go to the concert, but that didn't matter to Victor. So far as he was concerned, any opposition she might raise to his plans was purely negligible.

She was ready when Victor arrived that evening, dressed in a plain gown of purple wool that did not enhance her colouring. But it was a dress Victor had brought back from Italy after a business trip and she knew he expected her to wear it whenever she could. The black cape she wore with it was more becoming, but as her hair was confined in a knot at the nape of her neck, she still managed to look staid and matronly. Was this to be her role in life? she had asked herself as her fingers trembled fastening the zip of her dress. Constantly aware of the age gap between herself and Victor and his obvious attempts to close it in this way?

The Festival Hall was almost full when they arrived and as Emma had not examined the tickets Victor had been given she was unaware that their seats would be in the front row until they were shown into them. Her heart pounded heavily. Surely Miguel could not fail to see her from this distance if he chose to look. She sighed. Why should Victor have been given such exceptionally good tickets? Surely they would have had no difficulty in selling these seats when almost all the hall was full. She moved uncomfortably. Had Victor in fact bought these tickets especially because he knew she liked the music and only pretended they were complimentary? She glanced at her fiancé uncertainly. If he had done so, then she should feel grateful and not resentful at all.

The orchestra leader came in to a loud burst of applause and after several minutes interval the conductor appeared. Emma waited tensely for the soloist. There was a grand piano waiting for him, a beautiful instrument, sleek and highly polished. Like the performer, thought Emma, with a rising sense of hysteria.

And then Miguel Salvaje came out and weakness flooded her being. Tall, lean; his immaculate evening clothes complemented his dark alien attractiveness, and Emma sank down in her seat, praying he would not notice her.

He seated himself at the piano, the applause died, and Miguel began the introduction to Rachmaninov's second piano concerto. There was absolute silence in the hall, and Emma found her initial nervousness dispersing under the pure delight of the music. It was obvious that Miguel was interested only in the instrument under his hands, and his mastery cast a spell over the audience so that when it was over there was a moment's spellbound silence before the applause broke out. Emma found herself applauding just as enthusiastically, and only when he rose from the piano stool to take his bow and his gaze flickered over the front row did she realize Miguel had known she was there all the time. There was no element of surprise in the depths of his dark eyes, but they moved away before she could register any acknowledgment of that brief appraisal.

However, afterwards she had reason to doubt the truth of her earlier beliefs. At no time during the remainder of the evening did his eyes turn in her direction, and she began to wonder whether she had imagined the whole thing. But she had not been mistaken, she told herself angrily. He had seen her, but whether he had actually been aware of her presence beforehand, she was less positive.

Victor enjoyed the concert without any of Emma's misgivings. Unaware of his fiancée's mental agitation, he could not understand the unusual pallor of her cheeks as they left the auditorium, and suggested that instead of having supper out they should go back to his service apartment and eat there.

But Emma felt that food of any kind would choke her. Forcing a polite smile, she said: 'I don't think that's a very good idea, Victor. Perhaps if you took me home, Mrs. Cook

38

could make us some sandwiches . . .'

Victor hesitated, his square face showing his perplexity. Exhaling his breath noisily, he eventually nodded. 'Oh, very well, then. But I only had a sandwich before the concert, and I'm quite peckish.'

Emma tucked her skirts about her as she got into Victor's luxurious limousine. 'I'm sure we can find something,' she observed comfortingly, and Victor nodded without enthusiasm.

In fact, Mrs. Cook was out when they arrived back at the house. Emma realized the housekeeper would not have expected them back so early, and hiding her weariness she made Victor comfortable in the lounge with a drink and then went herself into the kitchen to prepare the food.

There was plenty to choose from: cold ham, plenty of bacon and eggs, salad, a cold meat pie. Deciding Victor would prefer something hot, Emma decided to make a cheese omelette, and she was beating eggs in the pan when the telephone rang.

Frowning, she waited a moment to see if Victor would answer it, and when he did not, she dried her fingers on a cloth and went out into the hall. Lifting the receiver, she gave her number, wondering who could possibly be ringing at this hour of the evening.

'Hello, Emma!'

The deep accented male voice was instantly recognizable and she almost dropped the receiver from her nerveless fingers.

'Y – yes, *señor*?' she murmured huskily.

'You enjoyed the concert, *si*?'

Any doubts she had had about his possible recognition of her presence fled away. 'Yes, thank you,' she answered, stiffly, politely. 'You played brilliantly.'

'*Gracias, señorita!*' There was a trace of mockery in his tones. 'I was sure your – fiancé – would use the tickets.'

'You were sure – you mean—' Emma broke off, breathing jerkily. 'You sent Victor those tickets?'

'But of course. Did you think otherwise?'

Emma glanced at the lounge door. It was closed, but she could not be sure that Victor could not overhear what she was saying. A pulse pounded heavily in her forehead, and her palms were moist. 'I – I didn't realize,' she managed unevenly.

'But you came.'

'Naturally.' She infused a tone of indifference. 'Why not? Was that why you rang? To find out whether I enjoyed it?'

There was silence for a long moment, and she thought with an awful feeling of bereavement that he had hung up on her. Then he said in a quiet voice: 'No, I rang because I wanted to speak with you, to hear your voice. I want to see you, Emma.'

Emma's legs turned to jelly beneath her. 'I'm afraid I can't talk now,' she said uneasily.

'Does that mean that you wish to talk at some other time?' he queried lazily. 'I gather the worthy Señor Harrison is there.'

'How do you—' she lowered her voice – 'how do you know my fiancé's name?'

'I made it my business to find out.' He hesitated a moment. 'Will he be gone soon?'

'Why?'

'I've told you. I want to see you.'

'Tonight?' Emma was horrified.

'Why not? Tomorrow I have a rehearsal and another concert. My time is limited.'

'I'm afraid that's impossible,' she exclaimed, glancing again towards the lounge door.

'Why is it impossible? Unless . . .' his voice cooled perceptibly . . . 'you sleep with this man Harrison—'

40

'Of course not!' Emma was furious. 'I don't sleep with anyone!'

'No?' His accent was very pronounced suddenly. 'What time will he leave?'

The lounge door suddenly opened, and Victor's broad frame filled the aperture. 'What's going on?' he demanded, sniffing strongly. 'Is something burning?'

'Oh, heavens, the omelette!' Emma looked down at the phone helplessly, and Victor made an angry gesture.

'Who is it?'

Emma put the receiver to her ear. 'I can't talk any more now – J-Jennifer. C-could you ring tomorrow?'

Without waiting for Miguel's reply, she thrust the receiver down on the rest and fled into the kitchen, grabbing the smoking pan from the flame. The eggs were ruined, a brown and lumpy mess in the bottom of the pan.

Victor had followed her and looked over her shoulder critically. Wrinkling his nose at the remains of the omelette, he said: 'Who's Jennifer?'

'Jennifer?' Emma sought wildly for an explanation. 'You remember Jennifer. She – she and I used to be great friends before she got married.'

'I thought that was Sheila.'

'I did have more than one friend,' retorted Emma, with an amazing amount of composure in the circumstances. She looked down into the pan. 'Go and sit down again, and I'll make another omelette.'

'No, thanks.' Victor stretched his arms tiredly. 'Quite honestly, after waiting so long my appetite's somewhat diminished.'

Emma bit her lip. 'I'm sorry.'

'So'm I.' Victor turned and walked back into the hall. 'I'll just finish my drink and then I'll go. You look tired. Aren't you sleeping well?'

Emma moved her head helplessly. 'Reasonably well,' she

answered. She followed him into the lounge. 'At least let me get you another drink.'

'No, thanks. I've had enough. I have to drive home, remember?'

Emma nodded and stood uncertainly, twisting her hands together as he swallowed the remains of his Scotch.

'What did she want anyway?' Victor returned to the subject of the phone call and Emma who had thought that matter over made a deprecatory gesture.

'Oh, she'd tried to ring me earlier, and when I wasn't in, she decided to ring back.'

'Was it something important?'

Emma managed a smile, feeling the guilt burning in her cheeks. 'Not really. She's – expecting her first baby.' That was an inspiration and seemed to satisfy Victor at last.

'Oh, well, I must go.' He came towards her, taking her by the shoulders and holding her firmly as he bent to kiss her lips. It was meant to be a very chaste kiss, but Emma, disturbed and needing reassurance, allowed her lips to part beneath his, pressing closer against him.

Victor drew back at once, taking a handkerchief from his pocket and wiping his mouth rather vigorously. 'I must go,' he said, his face flushed for once. 'Good night, Emma.'

'Good night, Victor.'

Emma pressed her lips together and accompanied him to the door. If only he showed a little more emotion! Heavens, they were to be married soon. What kind of a relationship were they going to have if he backed away from the most natural demonstrations of their love for one another?

Victor didn't kiss her again. He squeezed her hand warmly, and then went down the steps. Emma closed the door with a kind of suppressed violence, wishing for the first time in her life that she had a little more experience where men were concerned.

She had just finished cleaning up the kitchen when Mrs.

Cook returned. The housekeeper came into the room looking in surprise at the scoured pan. 'What happened?' she asked. 'I thought you were eating out.'

Emma had not told Mrs. Cook they were going to the Salvaje concert. It was easier that way.

'We were,' she answered her now. 'But I wasn't very hungry, so we came back here.'

'So I see.' Mrs. Cook took off her coat and went to hang it away. Emma realized she had accepted the explanation without elaboration and decided to say no more. There was no point in relating the circumstances which had led up to the present state of affairs unless she wanted to make more explanations. Instead, she said good night, and went up to bed.

But although she was tired, sleep was elusive. She kept wondering what Miguel Salvaje had thought of her abrupt ending of their telephone conversation. She was half prepared to believe that he might indeed come round to the house, but the dawn light was paling the sky when she at last fell into a deep slumber and no one had disturbed the silence of the night.

Mrs. Cook awoke her at ten with a cup of tea. Regarding Emma's pale face critically, she said: 'You look terrible! Didn't you sleep?'

Emma struggled up and took the cup of tea. 'Not very well,' she conceded, pushing back her heavy hair. 'What time is it?'

'Ten o'clock. Do you want breakfast in bed?'

Emma grimaced. 'No, nothing, thank you.'

Mrs. Cook shrugged and walked towards the door. Then she halted. 'By the way, there was a telephone call for you.'

Emma's nerves tightened. 'Already?'

'Yes. That Miss Harding from the agency. She said to ask you whether you could go in this afternoon. Apparently she's

43

short-staffed again.'

'Oh!' Emma put down her cup and lay back against the pillows. 'Oh, yes, I suppose I could. Was that all?'

'What more did you expect?' Mrs. Cook was curious.

Emma shook her head. 'Oh, nothing.'

'Did you enjoy the concert last evening?'

Emma stared at her. 'How do you know we went to a concert?'

'Miss Harding told me. When I told her you were still in bed she asked whether you'd had a late evening.'

'I see.' Emma swung her legs out of bed and reached for her dressing gown. 'Oh, well, it was no secret.'

'Then why didn't you tell me?' Mrs. Cook folded her arms. 'Does Mr. Harrison know that Salvaje brought you home the night of the fog and then visited here a week later?'

Emma rose to her feet. 'No, why should he?'

'Strange that he should buy tickets for that particular performer, don't you think?'

Emma gave an exasperated sigh. 'You're an inquisitive old woman, Mrs. Cook!'

'I know it. I also know that while your father's away I'm responsible for you.'

'I'm twenty-five, Mrs. Cook!'

'I know that. But you're still my responsibility. If you ask me, there's something peculiar about the whole thing.'

'Nobody asked you, Mrs. Cook.'

The housekeeper sighed and her expression became anxious. 'Miss Emma! You wouldn't be thinking of doing anything silly now, would you?'

'I don't know what you mean.' Emma moved towards her. 'Make me some coffee, there's a love. I'm not hungry, but I could certainly enjoy some of your coffee.'

Mrs. Cook moved aside reluctantly. 'Oh, all right. Are you going to ring Miss Harding? She asked if you could ring

44

her back.'

Emma nodded. 'Yes, I'll give her a ring.'

She waited for Mrs. Cook to move out on to the landing and then she passed her on her way to the bathroom. She knew the housekeeper suspected there was more to this than she could possibly know, but now that she had learned about the concert what more could Emma tell her? There was nothing more.

Emma was in her bedroom, brushing her hair, when the doorbell rang. There was nothing unusual in that. Trades-people were always calling. But when Mrs. Cook came to the foot of the stairs and called up to her, her heart began to thump a little more vigorously.

'Miss Emma! There's someone here to see you.'

Emma rose to her feet, looking helplessly at her unbound hair. It would take ages to fold it into its pleat, so she hastily plaited it into a thick braid and secured it with an elastic band. Her suit looked rather ridiculous with the childish hair-style, but it would have to do.

She hurried down the stairs and then came to an abrupt halt when she saw Miguel Salvaje standing below her. She wanted to turn and dash back up the stairs again, but he had heard her and swung round to face her.

'Good morning, *señorita*,' he greeted her, gallantly bowing his head, and Emma took a deep breath and de-scended the rest of the stairs.

'Good morning, *señor*.'

Not one would have recognized the elegantly attired soloist of the night before as this casually dressed stranger. Close-fitting denim jeans topped by a navy roll-necked sweater and a waist-length denim jerkin disguised him most effectively, and he could have been taken for a student.

'You are surprised to see me?' he inquired, in his lazy accented voice.

Emma shook her head slowly. 'N-not entirely,' she admit-

45

ted. 'But—' she glanced round to make sure Mrs. Cook was not hovering in the background, 'I thought you had a rehearsal today.'

He tipped his head on one side. 'I did. I do. But I am afraid I am – how do you say it – playing truant? *Si?*'

'*Si.*' Emma made a helpless gesture. 'Why have you come?'

'Ah!' he shrugged. 'Are you going to offer me some of that excellent coffee I can smell from the kitchen?'

Emma hesitated. 'Well, I suppose so.' She crossed the hall and thrust open the lounge door with rather jerky movements. 'If – if you'll go in there and wait, I'll speak to Mrs. Cook.'

'Very well.' He did as she had suggested and with an exasperated shrug Emma hastened down the hall.

Mrs. Cook was busy at the sink and she looked up reprovingly as Emma entered the room. 'Well?' she said. 'Has he gone?'

'No.' Emma looked at the percolator bubbling on the stove. 'He – er – do you think we could have some coffee?'

Mrs. Cook dried her hands. 'I expect so.' But her tone was not encouraging.

Emma sighed. 'Don't look so – well, disapproving, Mrs. Cook. Why shouldn't I offer him coffee?'.

'Well, as you've asked me, I should have thought the reasons were obvious. Why is he here? What does he want?'

Emma set cups on a tray. 'I don't know,' she replied rather sharply. 'Perhaps he wants to ask me if I enjoyed the concert.'

Mrs. Cook gave her an old-fashioned look. 'Oh, yes! I suppose he visits all his patrons and asks them that!'

'All right, all right. I suppose he wanted to see me.' Emma was resigned.

'Why?'

46

'I don't know.'

'Don't you?'

'No.' Emma picked up the tray. 'Is this everything?'

'Unless you want biscuits.'

'No, I don't think so. Thank you.'

Emma carried the tray along to the lounge and entering found Miguel seated at the piano, playing very softly. But he stopped when she came in, and rising to his feet took the tray from her hands and placed it on the low table in front of the fire.

Emma subsided rather thankfully on to the couch beside the table and trying to control her unsteady hands, asked: 'Cream and sugar?'

'No. Black, please.' He came to sit beside her on the couch, stretching out his long legs in front of him, resting his head back against the soft leather upholstery. 'Hmm, this is very nice. Much nicer than a cold concert hall.'

Emma placed his cup of coffee on the table near him and then busied herself pouring some for herself. But she was conscious of him only inches away from her, and of the lean brown hand with its carved gold ring lying on the couch between them. His fingers were long; artistic, and yet masculine, the silky dark hairs on the back of his hand signifying its strength.

Emma lifted her cup and swallowed a mouthful of coffee without thinking, almost scalding herself in the process. She coughed, apologized, and then replaced her cup on the tray.

'You are so nervous, Emma,' he remarked lazily. 'Why? What are you afraid of? Me?'

'Of course not.' Emma straightened her shoulders. 'Er – what are you playing this evening?'

'I do not want to talk about my work,' he stated briefly, and she identified the note of impatience that had suddenly entered his voice. Then, softening, he went on: 'Have you looked outside? It is one of your English autumn days that makes one feel glad to be alive.'

Emma glanced towards the windows. She could see what he meant. Pale golden sunlight was spilling over the stark bareness of the trees in the garden, gilding the dew-wet spiders' webs with an unearthly jewel-like fragility. Even the pale colours of autumn were magically strengthened, and although she knew the air would be cold, Emma guessed it was as clear and fresh as good wine.

'I want to be out in the day,' he said quietly. 'I want to drive to the coast, and feel the cold wind from the sea on my face. I want to feel free again!' He stretched out a hand and tugged gently at her braid which hung almost to her waist. 'And I want you to come with me!'

Emma trembled. 'That – that's impossible, I'm afraid—' she began, when his face darkened ominously.

'Why? Why is it impossible? Always you say this to me! It is not impossible! Nothing is impossible! And what is more, I will not accept any more excuses from you!'

He had straightened from his lounging position and was glaring at her angrily, and Emma found her breathing somewhat constricted by that close scrutiny. But trying not to be intimidated, she said: 'I am not making excuses, *señor*. I work in a secretarial agency, and I'm due there in a little under two hours.'

He flung himself off the couch and away from her, thrusting his hands into the pockets of his jeans. 'A secretarial agency,' he muttered grimly. Then he turned to look at her. 'And this is your final word?'

Emma rose nervously to her feet, clasping her hands in front of her. 'I – I – what more can I say, *señor*?'

'My name is Miguel,' he muttered broodingly, regarding her with a mixture of exasperation and malevolence.

Emma returned his gaze for a few moments, but then her lids dropped defensively before the intensity of his eyes. He remained staring at her for a while longer, and then he crossed the room to stand in front of her. Putting out a hand he lifted her chin, and her eyes flickered open. 'Come with me, Emma,' he murmured appealingly.

Although his fingers were cool, they burned her flesh where they touched, and she jerked away from him. 'I can't.'

'You mean you daren't,' he returned bitterly.

Emma took a deep breath. 'You place a very high value on your company, *señor*,' she snapped. 'I can assure you—'

But Miguel was reaching for her, his hands on her shoulders, impelling her towards him. 'Be silent!' he muttered impatiently, and bending his head he fastened his mouth on hers with devastating possession.

Emma struggled impotently for a few moments, but the hard muscles of his chest imprisoned her hands and they fluttered like birds trapped in a snare. His mouth hardened deliberately as she struggled and Emma felt her lips parting almost without volition. An awful weakness flooded her, all resistance ebbing away. His hands slid down her back to her hips, holding her firmly against him so that she was made aware of every muscle of his thighs. No one, least of all Victor, had ever kissed her so long or so thoroughly, and when at last he lifted his head she felt a sense of loss and dissatisfaction, as though her body yearned for a fulfilment it had not received.

But like a drowning man coming to the surface, sanity brought a sense of shame and humiliation, and although he did not move away when his hands fell to his sides she stepped several paces backward.

Miguel took a long narrow cigar out of his pocket and placing it between his teeth proceeded to light it with calm deliberation. 'Stop looking as though I have seduced you,' he remarked lazily. 'For a woman of twenty-five, you're remarkably inexperienced.'

49

Emma gathered her scattered senses. 'I'm sorry,' she replied stiffly. 'But I didn't ask you to find out.'

The corners of his thin mouth lifted. 'No. But you didn't object either, did you?'

Emma uttered a gasp and turned away, pressing the palms of her hands to her burning cheeks, and with an exclamation he said: 'Emma! Don't make such a thing of it. Now, go and get changed, and we'll go to the coast!'

Emma swung round. 'Do you think I'd go out with you after this?' she demanded in astonishment.

Miguel's face darkened. 'I don't think anything, Emma. I know it!'

'You can't make me!'

'Can't I?' His eyes narrowed.

Emma shook her head a trifle confusedly. 'Why do you want to take *me*?'

'Because I enjoy your company.'

'But there must be other women – I mean – I'm sure I'm not the only woman you know in London.'

'I don't – know – you yet, Emma,' he replied disturbingly.

Emma took a shaking breath. 'But I'm not your type. And besides, there's Victor.'

'You want I should invite him also?' Miguel raised his dark brows and Emma had to shake her head slowly. 'So! Get ready. And please – wear something less – less unattractive.' He flicked his fingers at the suit as though it offended him. 'Don't you have any trousers?'

Emma hesitated. 'I – I have an old pair of jeans,' she faltered.

'Good. Don't be long.'

And with that he turned his back on her and walked over to the piano. She left the room with the plaintive sound of lyrical pastoral music which she recognized as Grieg's filling her ears. Obviously, though he refused to discuss his music, it was terribly important to him. No one could coax such gentle melancholy, such compassion, from an instrument without awareness of the deep correlation between them. She had never experienced such a surging of emotion as was emanating from the keys, and she went out quickly and closed the door.

But in the hall, a chill feeling of apprehension settled upon her. What was she thinking of, allowing him to direct her movements like this? What did she know about him after all? His relationships, his background, his way of life? He could be married for all she knew, and very likely was. And what about Victor, and her job at the agency?

Mrs. Cook came out of the kitchen and saw her standing there. 'Is something wrong?' she asked, a look of concern on her face.

Emma sighed. 'No, nothing's wrong, Mrs. Cook. I – er – I'm going out. With – with Señor Salvaje.'

Mrs. Cook looked horrified. 'But I thought – that is – you rang Miss Harding and told her you would go in to work.'

'I did. But I shall ring again and tell her I can't.'

Mrs. Cook shook her head, obviously confused and worried. 'And what will you tell her? That you're going out with this – this piano-player!'

Emma's lips curved in an unwilling smile. No one could call Miguel Salvaje just a piano-player. It was sacrilegious! But she didn't contradict her.

'No,' she answered now. 'I shall tell her I've got a headache.'

Mrs. Cook folded her arms. 'And Mr. Harrison? What about him?'

'Oh, I'm not seeing Victor until tonight. Besides, I shall be back some time this afternoon, I expect. Mig – that is – Señor Salvaje – has a recital this evening.'

Mrs. Cook could not have looked more disapproving. 'I don't know,' she exclaimed. 'Telling lies to Miss Harding, going out with another man behind Mr. Harrison's back! What's got into you?'

Emma bent her head. 'Nothing's got into me, Mrs. Cook. Good heavens, you're behaving as though I was planning to run away with the man! We're only driving to the coast. What harm is there in that?'

Mrs. Cook shrugged. "You know the answer to that as well as I do,' she retorted. 'Have sense, girl! What's a man like him troubling with you for, if it's not for – well, the obvious reasons!'

Emma clenched her fists. Mrs. Cook was voicing all her own fears and apprehensions and right now she didn't want to listen to them.

'I've got to go,' she said shortly. 'I need to change, and I don't have time to argue about it any longer. I'm sorry if you don't approve, but I'm still going.'

Mrs. Cook made an eloquent gesture as though washing her hands of the whole business and Emma walked quickly back along the hall and up the stairs to her room.

Maybe she was being foolish, behaving like an infatuated schoolgirl with a man who was obviously experienced in the ways of her sex. But everyone was entitled to be foolish at some time in their lives, and this was her moment, and no one else's.

CHAPTER FOUR

THE jeans had been bought several years ago before Emma's lean young flanks had filled out, and now they felt absurdly tight and clinging. But as she took in her appearance while fastening the buttons of the turquoise cotton shirt she had chosen to wear with them, she realized they suited her. The shirt, long-sleeved and masculine with a severely cut suit, acquired different characteristics when matched with the jeans, and her reflection in the mirror startled her somewhat. She looked attractive, and young, and wholly unlike the Emma she had grown used to seeing over the years.

Only her hair caused her some misgivings, but finally she divided it and plaited it and bound it round her head in a coronet of braids. She hesitated about make-up, but eventually used only a faint eye-shadow and a colourless lustre that one of the girls at the agency had given her on her last birthday in an effort to show her what cosmetics she ought to use.

She descended the stairs as quietly as possible. She hoped Mrs. Cook would not emerge from her kitchen until they had gone, but as she extracted her sheepskin jacket from the hall closet, the housekeeper reappeared.

For several minutes she just looked at Emma, causing the bright colour to flood her cheeks, and then she said in a scandalized voice: 'You're not going out like that!'

'Why not?' Emma managed to sound nonchalant.

'Those trousers – they're practically indecent! Miss Emma, your father would be most upset if he knew.'

Emma sighed. 'But he doesn't know, does he? And in any case, I'm well past the age of consent, Mrs. Cook.'

'Yes, miss.'

Emma sighed again. 'Mrs. Cook, try to understand how I feel. I've never – well, for years there's been only Victor. Surely everyone is entitled to a bit of freedom now and then.'

Mrs. Cook shook her head. 'I can't stop you. It's your life.'

'Yes. Yes, it is, isn't it?' Emma gave her one last appealing look and then walked down the hall to the lounge door. When she looked back, however, Mrs. Cook had gone into the kitchen again.

There was no sound from the piano now, and when she entered the room she found Miguel stretched out lazily on the couch, his eyes closed. He looked completely at home there, as Victor had never done, and her heart lurched sickeningly. She was crazy allowing him to get any small foothold in her life. It could only cause her heartbreak in the end.

She had thought at first he was asleep, but as she moved further into the room, his eyes flickered open and alighted on her. Then he swung his booted feet to the ground and got to his feet.

'You're ready?' he inquired casually.

Emma nodded, her throat tight. If her appearance had caused some reaction with Mrs. Cook, it certainly did not appear to surprise Miguel Salvaje. She almost felt disappointed, but then he was holding open the door for her and slipping on her sheepskin coat she preceded him outside.

The Jensen awaited them at the bottom of the drive, sleek and latently powerful. Seeing him beside his car made Emma realize how great was the gulf between them. He might look like a student, but his potential was vastly superior. And yet he treated the vehicle with the same casual indifference he assumed towards his music. It was apparent that possessions were not a particular source of pleasure to him.

54

He unlocked the passenger side door and Emma got quickly inside. Miguel walked round and climbed in beside her, and without wasting any more time started the engine. There was a low roar and they moved forward, out of Dudley Gardens into the main stream of traffic.

Emma tried to relax. She was committed now, so she might as well make the best of it. There was the same warm, luxurious smell in the car as there had been the night he had driven her home. Leather, and good tobacco, and what might have been shaving lotion. But it was daylight now and she was able to see the refinements of the vehicle. Not even Victor's opulent limousine boasted a cassette recorder or a refrigerated cabinet.

Miguel didn't speak much. He was concentrating on the heavy traffic, manoeuvring the Jensen with smooth expertise, and Emma tried not to watch him. But it was difficult when her eyes were drawn to his frowning profile by the primitive strength of his magnetism.

But eventually the city was left behind, and the Jensen was allowed a little more freedom. It responded eagerly, obviously more at ease in the sixties and seventies than when its power was subdued to conform to speed regulations.

Emma looked across at her companion. Although the traffic was less heavy now, Miguel seemed as absorbed as ever, and with a nervous cough, she said: 'Where are we going?'

Miguel roused himself with obvious difficulty. 'Well, where do you think we are going?' he parried.

Emma shrugged. 'We're on the Brighton road. Are we going there?'

Miguel drew in his lower lip with his teeth. 'I do not know these places well. My London agent took me there once, but I thought there might be somewhere out of town where we might just walk.'

Emma nodded. 'It's possible to walk from Brighton to

Worthing,' she agreed. 'We could do that, although—'

'Although?' he pressed her.

'I was thinking of the time factor,' she replied. 'Don't you have to be back in London—'

'Leave me to concern myself with my affairs,' he snapped shortly, and Emma shrank back in her seat.

For a time there was silence and Emma knew she would not be the one to break it this time. She didn't understand him. At the house he had been so – so different, somehow. Approachable, appealing, attractive. Now he was silent and morose, engrossed with his own thoughts.

Brighton was quiet on this rather windy November day. The wind was off the sea, and chilling in its intensity. Emma was glad of her sheepskin jacket which she wrapped tightly about her, and Miguel pulled a fur-lined jacket from the back of the car and put it on. It was black and accentuated his darkness, that alien quality about him. Emma began to wish she had never agreed to come.

He parked the car, and after locking it, glanced at his wrist watch. 'It's almost one o'clock,' he remarked. 'Shall we have some lunch?'

Emma, who had had no breakfast, was beginning to feel rather empty, but the idea of sitting in a restaurant with him, constantly afraid of recognition appalled her.

'I – er – a sandwich would do for me,' she volunteered awkwardly.

Miguel regarded her dourly. 'Why? Don't you normally eat lunch? You don't look to me as though you have to consider your diet.'

Emma sighed. 'I thought you'd rather have a sandwich at a snack bar than risk being identified in some restaurant.'

'Why should I care about being identified?'

Emma made a helpless gesture. 'The last time you asked me to eat with you, you said—'

'I know what I said.' The planes of his face were shad-

56

owed. 'Nevertheless, we will have a meal.'

Emma made no comment and he indicated that they should walk out of the parking area and along the sea front. They walked together like strangers, and Emma thrust her hands into her pockets so that he should not think she wanted him to touch her. There was something vaguely melancholy about the day, as though Miguel's mood had overlaid it, and yet for all that, Emma knew that given the same circumstances, she would probably have done the same thing over again.

They had lunch in the restaurant of the Capricorn Hotel, one of the larger hotels on the sea front. The food was good, but Emma's appetite was not. In spite of feeling empty inside, she realized that the sensation was not wholly physical, and although she drank a little of the soup and managed to swallow several mouthfuls of the steak they had to follow, only the wine enabled her to get anything down. Miguel waived the soup, but seemed to enjoy the steak, and spoke for a while on the eating habits of his country. Emma was fascinated and encouraged when he spoke about his homeland, but when she ventured to question him on a more personal level he closed up like a clam and said no more. She came to the conclusion that he was an intensely moody person, and felt irritated that it could upset her so.

Afterwards, they came out into the cold air, and crossing the road went down on to the shingly beach. Miguel scuffed his suede boots in the stones and stared out to sea. It was a grey sea, lightened only by the fading brilliance of the sun, and he turned to look at Emma with sardonic eyes.

'So dull,' he said. 'So colourless. Have you ever seen the Pacific when the surf is running? Have you ever experienced the thrill of pitting your skill against the power of the ocean? Have you ever balanced on the crest of a wave and hurtled into shore at breathtaking speeds?'

Emma bent her head. 'You must know I haven't,' she

57

replied, rather shortly.

'How should I know that?' he countered mockingly. 'I know very little about you, Emma.'

'And I know even less about you,' retorted Emma, looking up, her eyes sparkling angrily.

'So?' He spread a casual hand. 'I am unimportant. Come! Let us walk.'

They walked in silence for some distance, climbing up from the beach to walk through grassy sand dunes where there was a little shelter from the wind. With the sinking of the sun, it was growing colder, and darker, and Emma wished she knew how much longer he intended to go on.

And then, as though sensing her unease, he halted and seated himself on a grassy slope overlooking the shingle. He took one of the long thin cigars he favoured from his pocket and sheltering his lighter lit it and inhaled deeply. Then he looked up at Emma, standing beside him, and indicated that she should sit down also.

Emma perched awkwardly on the slope beside him, drawing up her knees and wrapping her arms round them in an effort to keep warm.

'Hmm,' he said lazily. 'That is good. The air is good.'

'I thought you found it dull and colourless,' remarked Emma, not looking at him.

He shrugged. 'You find me difficult to understand, do you not, Emma?'

Emma hunched her shoulders. 'I suppose so.'

'Why? Because I do not conform to your ideas of what I should be?'

'I wouldn't presume to tell you what you should be,' retorted Emma stiffly, and he laughed.

'Why not? Because you do not always get the reactions you expect? Hmm?'

Emma shook her head. 'Do you realize it's after three o'clock and we're miles from the car?'

'Oh, Emma! Always you are so correct. Do you never – how do you say it – let go? Forget the time? Time is relative.'

'And if you don't get back to town in time for the recital?'

'I don't get back,' he replied calmly. 'Already I am in trouble for missing today's rehearsal. What does it matter if there is a little more trouble, hmm?'

Emma sighed, and he turned to look at her with disturbing intensity. 'You are disappointed, are you not?'

Emma raised her eyebrows in surprise. 'Disappointed?'

'Yes, disappointed. Because we have spoken so little; because I have used you merely as a companion, that is all.'

'I don't know what you mean.'

'Oh, yes. Oh, yes, Emma, you do. Agreeing to come out with me was a – daring – thing for someone like you to do, and now you feel it has all been a waste of time.'

'No!' Emma flushed.

'But yes. Do not be afraid to be honest with yourself.'

She wished he would stop staring at her. She felt almost sure he could see into her mind, so accurate was his assessment of her feelings. What *was* she doing here, she asked herself desperately, risking Victor's anger and her job at the agency?

Miguel trailed the back of his hand down one of her cold cheeks, allowing his fingers to stroke the side of her neck. His eyes were concealed behind the dark lashes so that she could not read the expression in their depths, but they held hers and like a rabbit in thrall she could not look away.

'Why do you scrape your hair back like this?' he demanded softly, pulling painfully at the loosened strands at the nape of her neck. 'Unfasten it for me!'

Emma put a defensive hand to her throat. 'Don't be silly!'

'I mean it. Do you want me to do it? I warn you – I might

not be very gentle.'

'I – I can't.'

He shrugged and without a word began to fumble with the braids, hurting her deliberately, she thought.

'All – all right, all right, I'll do it.' Emma swallowed convulsively, and bending her head began to take the securing hairpins from the coronet of plaits. They fell, one over each shoulder, and his eyes softened miraculously.

'Better, much better,' he murmured, and reaching out threaded his fingers through the one nearest to him, releasing its heavy silkiness.

Emma sat completely motionless, aware of his fingers in her hair but unable to look at him. She despised herself for allowing him to force her to do what he wanted, and yet there was an aching delight in his touch. Bending his head, he pressed a handful of her hair to his lips, and then increased the pressure so that she was forced to turn and look at him. She knew he was going to kiss her again, and she uttered a little cry of protest which he completely ignored. His mouth moved on hers with gentle insistence that disarmed her so that her lips parted involuntarily. But when he felt her response, something seemed to snap within him, and his mouth hardened to a passionate demand. Her face was imprisoned between his hands and she lost her balance and fell back against the sandy grass, the weight of his body almost knocking the breath out of hers.

She put up her hands in an effort to push him away, but they betrayed her, sliding round his neck, tangling themselves in his hair, clinging to him. She felt him unbuttoning her jacket and his own so that presently only the thickness of her blouse and his sweater was between them. They were cocooned in an aura of warmth and intimacy, but when his hands separated her blouse from the waistband of her jeans and slid next to her warm flesh, Emma dragged her mouth away from his, turning her face urgently from side to side.

'No,' she said imploringly, 'no! Please – *don't*!'

'Why?' he murmured into her neck, his breath warm on her soft skin. 'Don't you want me to touch you?'

Emma was panting now, as much with the fight against her own yielding senses as with the need to stop him. 'Miguel – please!' she breathed weakly. 'Let me go!'

He went suddenly still, and without a word rolled away from her, and only then did she realize how cold it really was, and how dark it had become in those few minutes. He got to his feet, buttoning his jacket and smoothing his hair with a careless hand. Emma stood up too, but she felt terribly dishevelled, her hair in wild disorder about her face. Trying to gauge his mood, she looked nervously at him, but he was staring out to sea, his face dark and sombre, and she could not tell what he was thinking. Unable to prevent herself, she stammered: 'Are – you angry with me?'

He turned to look at her in the gloom. 'Why should I be angry with you?' he asked, without rancour.

Emma sighed. 'Well, I just – I thought—'

He moved towards her and began to fasten the leather buttons of her sheepskin jacket, drawing her closer to him as he did so, a faint smile lifting the corners of his mouth.

'Oh, Emma,' he said softly. 'Do you believe you could have stopped me just now if I had chosen to deprive you of your virginity?' Her cheeks flamed, and he went on: 'For you are a virgin, aren't you? I do have some small knowledge of your sex, you know.'

Emma shivered, and he slid an arm around her shoulders. 'Come along,' he said. 'It's getting late, and I do not want you to catch a chill.'

The walk back to the car was accomplished almost in silence and not until they were on the London road did he speak again, and then only to ask if she was warmer now.

They seemed to get back to town so much more quickly than they left, and Emma found herself dreading the moment when he would deposit her at her gate and drive away. She didn't want to leave him, and the knowledge that she might never see him again was tearing her apart. She didn't know what was the matter with her. She had never felt this way with Victor, and the prospect of the years ahead stretched cold and lifeless. Oh, God, she thought despairingly, what was happening to her?

The evening rush hour had begun by the time they reached the suburbs, but as most of the traffic was leaving the city, they drove through almost without incident. Miguel brought the Jensen to a smooth halt at the foot of her drive, and Emma gathered all her composure to say goodbye. But when she turned to him, he was smiling. He lifted one of her cold hands from her lap and raising it to his lips pressed his mouth to her palm.

'Thank you,' he said, his accent rather pronounced suddenly. 'And now I must go. Castillo, my manager, will be having – what is it? Cats? Kittens?'

'Kittens,' said Emma automatically.

'Ah, yes, kittens,' Miguel nodded. 'No matter. He will recover.'

Emma drew her fingers out of his grasp and fumbled for the door catch, but she couldn't find it, and she sighed impatiently. She was conscious of the prick of tears behind her eyes, and she wanted to get away from him before she made an absolute fool of herself.

Miguel thrust open his door, however, and climbing out walked round to swing open her door with a flourish. Emma scrambled out, stumbling over the rim in her haste, so that he had to save her from falling, grasping her wrists with his strong hands. But his brows drew together as he looked down into her pale face with sudden comprehension. Retaining his hold on her wrists, he demanded: 'What is it? What is wrong? Why do you look so – so *ansiosa*?'

Emma shook her head mutely, not trusting herself to

speak, and with an exclamation he went on: 'It is I? Something I have done?'

Emma managed a faint: 'No,' but he was unconvinced.

'You are sorry you came with me? You have not enjoyed yourself?'

Emma looked up. 'It – it's nothing, really!'

Miguel compressed his lips impatiently. 'I do not believe you, but I do not have the time right now to discover what it is that is troubling you. It will have to wait until later.'

Emma gasped, 'Later?'

'*Si*. After the concert. I will come back.'

'No – that is – you can't!'

'Why can't I?' There was a trace of arrogance in his voice now.

'I – Victor – will be here.'

Miguel shrugged. 'So? I am not afraid to meet Señor Harrison.'

'You don't understand. He wouldn't – understand – this!'

'So? Sooner or later it will not matter what he thinks.' He sighed, looking down at her slim wrists imprisoned within his hands. 'Emma, Castillo will be pacing the floor like a caged mountain lion! We will talk later, *si*?'

Emma shook her head slowly. Ever since she had got out of the car a sense of coldness had been invading her lower limbs, which was not completely attributable to the weather. Today had been a day out of time, but tomorrow, and all her tomorrows, belonged to Victor. She was fooling herself if she imagined that just because Miguel Salvaje was temporarily diverted by her companionship it was going to make any fundamental difference to her life. By bringing Victor into this she was gambling with her future, and when, in a couple of weeks or so, Miguel left for some other European capital to continue his concert tour she would be left to pick up the pieces.

Miguel stared down at her, a frustrated gleam of anger in his eyes. 'Emma! I have to go. Don't be like this.'

'Like what?' Emma managed to infuse a note of surprise into her voice. 'I – thank you for – for the day. I've enjoyed it. Good-bye.'

Miguel flung her hands away from him and muttering an epithet to himself strode away round the Jensen, sliding inside with unconcealed impatience. The engine roared, and seconds later it tore away, an angry whine in the distance.

Emma watched it until it was out of sight and then, turning, walked disconsolately up the drive, tugging at a strand of hair over her shoulder. Feeling her hair made her realize its state of disorder, and with fumbling fingers she endeavoured to secure it in a roll on the nape of her neck. But she knew it was useless, and she thrust open the door with some misgivings. Mrs. Cook would be bound to think the worst, and who could blame her?

As soon as she heard the door, Mrs. Cook came out of the kitchen, and the worried look on her face was there even before she took in Emma's dishevelled appearance. Emma endeavoured to smile, and said, unnecessarily: 'I'm back.'

Mrs. Cook came down the hall. 'Not before time,' she observed dryly.

'Why?'

'Mr. Harrison has been round here looking for you.'

Emma's lips parted. 'Victor?'

'Yes, that's right.'

'But what did he want?'

'You.' Mrs. Cook helped her off with her sheepskin coat and hung it away in the hall closet. 'He apparently went into the agency and—'

'—Fenella told him I was unwell,' Emma finished.

'More or less.'

'So what happened?'

Mrs. Cook gave a resigned sigh. 'I told him you were in

bed, *asleep*.'

Emma stared at her in relief. 'Oh, you darling!' she exclaimed. 'Thank you!'

'I didn't say he believed me,' said Mrs. Cook dourly.

'What do you mean?'

'Well, he said – if you were in bed, why weren't your bedroom curtains drawn?'

'He'd noticed, I suppose.'

'Naturally.'

'So what did you say?'

'I asked him if he was calling me a liar. He said not necessarily, so I asked him if he'd like to go up and see for himself.'

'Mrs. Cook!' Emma was aghast.

'I know. It was a bad moment, believe me! Anyway, it must have done the trick, because he said no, that's not necessary, and left.'

'Did – did he say when he'd be back?'

'Yes. He said he'd call this evening as planned.'

Emma heaved a sigh. 'Well, I'd better go upstairs and get washed and changed, hadn't I? And do something about my hair.'

Mrs. Cook folded her arms. 'Well? Was it worth it?'

Emma shrugged. 'Going out, you mean?' She made a deprecatory gesture. 'It was – all right.'

Mrs. Cook gave her a strange look. 'Are you seeing him again?'

'I doubt it.'

'Thank the Lord for that!' Mrs. Cook raised her eyebrows derisively, and marched off back into the kitchen. 'By the way,' she said as she opened the door, 'what time do you want to eat?'

'Whenever you like,' Emma replied, going up the stairs slowly. 'And, Mrs. Cook—'

'Yes?'

'Thanks again.'

Mrs. Cook snorted disapprovingly and went through the door, and Emma continued upstairs.

By the time Victor arrived Emma was dressed in a long black hostess gown and her hair was neatly confined in its pleat. She wore no jewellery, and felt as plain as she was sure she looked.

Victor came into the lounge after Mrs. Cook had admitted him, rubbing his hands together vigorously to warm them. Emma was seated on the couch and he bent to kiss her lightly on the forehead before taking up a position before the fire.

'Now then,' he said briskly, 'how are you feeling? I must say you look rather pale. Fenella was most concerned about you.'

Emma smoothed the skirt of her gown. 'I'm perfectly all right,' she answered. 'Help yourself to a drink, won't you?'

Victor frowned, but walked across to the drinks cabinet and poured himself a generous measure of Scotch. 'What will you have?'

Emma shook her head, indicating the coffee cups on the table. 'Nothing, thanks. Actually, Mrs. Cook brought two cups because she expected you a little earlier, but it's cold now, I'm afraid.'

'Yes.' Victor swallowed half his Scotch and came round the couch again. 'Well, I was held up at the office. This Messiter deal is taking longer than I expected.'

Emma forced herself to sound interested. 'You should delegate some of your work,' she said. 'There's no need for you to work the hours you do.'

Victor smiled. 'No, I realize that. And once we're married I intend to take things much easier.'

Ema's nerves tightened. 'I see.'

'We'll have to be thinking seriously of putting a date on

our wedding,' he went on. 'After all, once Christmas is over there's absolutely no need for delay. I thought perhaps February – or March. Your father will be back by then, won't he?'

Emma swallowed with difficulty. 'Oh, oh, yes. He – he expects to be back for Christmas, I think.'

'Does he?'

'Well, he wouldn't want me to be alone here over the festive season, I suppose—'

'Alone? You're not alone, Emma. You have me.'

'I know, I know.' Emma bit her lip. 'It's just that – well, Christmas is a time for families, isn't it?'

Victor shrugged his broad shoulders. 'I wouldn't know,' he replied. 'I've never had one.'

Emma was contrite. 'I'm sorry. I – I didn't mean—'

'I know you didn't.' Victor swallowed his drink, and then looked reflectively at her. 'Truth to tell, I've never cared for Christmas much. All that artificiality! Not for me.'

'But it needn't be, surely,' exclaimed Emma, in surprise. 'Why, when my mother was alive and my brother lived at home, we used to have marvellous Christmases.'

Victor looked bored by this turn of the conversation and regarding his empty glass, said: 'Can I get another?'

Emma nodded quickly. 'Of course. Just help yourself.'

'Thank you.'

Victor did so, and when he came back to his position by the fire he changed the conversation round to his present conflict with the board of Messiter Textiles. Emma listened while he gave a detailed explanation of their shortcomings and then went on to describe his plans for their future. Emma had heard it all before, but she tried to evince an interest she did not feel. Recollections of the day she had spent kept coming to cloud her awareness, and with them came visions of the years ahead and evenings like this when Victor would expect her to listen while he recounted the details of his day. There had to be more to marriage than this, she found herself thinking desperately. Perhaps if two people loved one another, if they shared a mutual understanding of one another, they became naturally involved with one another's lives. But she and Victor had a different kind of relationship. Emotion played a very small part, and while she admitted that a marriage based solely on sexual compatibility might not succeed, surely the physical side of their association should be a source of enjoyment to them.

But she couldn't imagine Victor enjoying anything where the subjugation of self was one of the prime factors. To picture Victor without his immaculate city clothes, without his armour of respectability, was like committing some sacrilegious act. She simply could not see him in that way.

Mrs. Cook brought in some sandwiches and coffee soon after ten o'clock, and Victor came to sit beside Emma on the couch so that he could reach the tray.

'By the way,' he said, munching on a ham roll, 'we're invited out to dinner on Friday evening.'

'Oh, yes?' Emma looked up. 'Who by?'

'The Hansons. You know – Miles and Delia. It's a kind of celebration really – their wedding anniversary. They've been married twenty-three years.' He shook his head. 'Imagine that! Soon be their silver wedding, won't it?'

Emma nodded, sipping her coffee without really tasting it. These people were Victor's friends, his contemporaries, and they were soon to be celebrating their silver wedding! Were they never to have any *young* friends, any friends of *her* age?

But no. She couldn't see Victor making conversation with any young man who had yet to make his way in the world. Such people bored him. His associates were all successful business men like himself, men who knew how to handle money, and people; though not always very considerately.

Victor smiled in a satisfied way as he drank his coffee.

'This is very nice, you know,' he said. 'I enjoy these evenings, just staying at home like this. Entertaining's all right, up to a point, but it's nice to relax, isn't it?'

Emma forced a faint smile to her lips. She hoped he would not stay late. The headache she had pretended earlier in the day was fast becoming a reality, and she longed for the oblivion of unconsciousness.

And then the doorbell rang, and her inertia fled, taking with it her peace of mind. She could think of no one who would call at this hour of the evening. No one, except . . .

Victor raised his eyebrows. 'Who's this?' he demanded gruffly.

Emma shook her head. 'I – I don't know,' she murmured, getting to her feet. 'I'll go and see.'

'Leave it to Mrs. Cook,' advised Victor, standing up too. 'Probably someone's got the wrong house.'

'Probably,' agreed Emma faintly, straining her ears to hear the housekeeper's steps along the hall, and presently the sound of the outer door being opened.

There was a moment's pregnant silence when she thought that Victor had been right, that someone had indeed got the wrong house, and then after a brief altercation in the hall the lounge door was summarily opened and Miguel stood in the aperture, Mrs. Cook hovering with nervous impotence behind him. Tall, lean, dark, dressed in a maroon velvet jacket over his evening shirt and trousers, he surveyed them both with mocking insolence.

'*Buenas noches, señor, señorita!*' he greeted them, bowing slightly. 'I trust I am not interrupting anything.'

CHAPTER FIVE

EMMA refused to look at Miguel after that first devastating recognition. She looked instead at Victor whose face was purpling in his confused efforts to find some reasonable explanation for this unexpected and unwanted intrusion. And in those few seconds she realized that her initial suspicions of Miguel's ruthlessness, of his complete lack of compunction about hurting people when it came to getting what he wanted, had been only too accurate. Watching Victor struggling to find words to break the ominous silence which had fallen was like watching the desperate antics of a fly who suddenly finds himself caught in a spider's web.

Then, as though realizing that she had said nothing, Victor turned to her and said: 'What's all this about, Emma? Do you know this man? Are you going to allow him to walk in here like this, uninvited and unannounced?'

Emma knew the onus was on her now. Picking her words carefully, she replied: 'I'm afraid there's been a mistake, Victor. Señor Salvaje called earlier and invited me to have supper with him. I refused, of course, but it seems he didn't understand.'

'Señor Salvaje!' Victor turned incredulously to Miguel. 'Dammit, do you mean to tell me you're that pianist – the one we saw last evening?'

Miguel inclined his head with sardonic politeness, and Victor shook his head a trifle bewilderedly. Then he looked at Emma again. 'And this man – Señor Salvaje – asked you out for supper this evening?' He was clearly flabbergasted.

Emma cast an appealing glance in Miguel's direction, silently begging for his support, but gained nothing from those enigmatic dark eyes. 'Y-yes,' she nodded now. 'That's right.'

Victor made a frustrated gesture. 'But why? Why you? Does he know you?'

Emma thought desperately. 'I – he – his manager supplied the agency with some work!' She hated involving Fenella like this, but surely if she explained the whole situation to her she would understand.

Victor frowned. 'I see. And I suppose Fenella gave him your address?'

Emma moved her shoulders helplessly. 'It's in the phone book.'

'Of course.' Victor snatched at this apparently sane piece of information like a drowning man reaching for straws. He turned to Miguel. 'I'm afraid I shall have to ask you to leave, *señor*. As you've heard from Miss Seaton herself, she does not wish to have supper with you, and if you understood otherwise, then it's most unfortunate.'

Miguel moved then, straightening from his lounging position and stepping into the room, closing the door gently but firmly in Mrs. Cook's face.

'I agree,' he said pleasantly, so that for a moment Emma thought everything was going to be all right. *But it wasn't!* 'It is unfortunate. But not for me, *señor*, for *you!*'

Victor straightened his shoulders and cleared his throat. 'I beg your pardon.'

'You heard what I said, *señor*.' Miguel was calm, but menacing.

'Miguel, *please*—' Emma's cry was damning in its implied intimacy and Victor gave her a startled look.

'You called him Miguel!' he exclaimed.

'Of course she did,' remarked Miguel coolly. 'Hasn't she told you we spent the day together?'

'*Miguel!*' Emma pressed both hands to her lips.

'Well? Didn't we?' His eyes challenged her.

71

Victor stared at her disbelievingly. 'Is this true, Emma?'

Emma's nostrils flared. 'And if it is?'

Victor's breathing was obviously forced. 'Are you telling me it is true?'

'Of course she is.' Miguel stood, arms folded, regarding them both with contemptuous eyes. 'Does it surprise you, Harrison, that your fiancée should find another man attractive? Surely you know enough about women to know how fickle they can be! You were married, weren't you? Didn't it teach you anything?'

'You're insolent, sir!' Victor's angry reproof was almost Victorian, and Emma shook her head helplessly.

'Please!' she exclaimed. 'Stop this!' She looked at Miguel in angry reproach. 'Why have you come here? What are you hoping to achieve by insulting us both like this?'

Miguel's hands dropped to his sides. 'I came to see you,' he replied simply. 'Didn't you want to see me?'

When he looked at her it was as though the two of them were alone in the room, and Emma's senses stirred unwillingly. But she dragged her gaze from his, moving her head vigorously from side to side. 'No!' she denied fiercely. 'No, I didn't ask you to come here.'

Miguel swore softly under his breath and stilled his immediate reaction to step towards her. Emma waited, motionless, for him to go, but instead he turned back to Victor. 'Well, *señor*?' he challenged. 'What are you going to do about it?'

'What am *I* going to do about it?' Victor was furious. '*Señor*, I don't like you, and I don't like your insinuations. If Emma – agreed to go out with you today then no doubt she had some good reason for doing so! I do not propose, however, to conduct any kind of question-and-answer session with my fiancée in front of you!'

Miguel's face darkened, and Emma mentally applauded

Victor's common sense. But it was short-lived. 'Your fiancée's reasons for coming out with me, *señor*, were excellent,' Miguel observed pleasantly. 'Shall I tell you what they were?' He raised his eyebrows mockingly. 'She is attracted to me, *señor*. She wanted me to make love to her!'

Emma's horrified gasp of: 'That's not true!' was stifled by Victor's enraged growl as he strode across the room to grasp the Mexican by his collar. But Miguel evaded his bull-like rush and sank his fist into Victor's solar plexus so that the older man uttered a groan and stood panting breathlessly.

'Oh, you – you swine!' cried Emma, rushing to Victor's side and endeavouring to help him into an armchair. 'How – how dare you?' She was trembling all over herself. If only she had not allowed herself to get involved with a man like him, she thought recriminatively. If she had only clung to her first assessment of him as a cruel and ruthless man; if only she had taken Mrs. Cook's advice and never allowed the situation to develop. She should have realized that she could not expect someone with a racial background of violence and savagery to conform to her standards.

Miguel regarded her with dislike. 'You are a hypocrite, Emma,' he stated coldly. 'You pretend an affection for this man when you know you do not love him. Can you honestly tell me I am wrong?'

Emma looked up from massaging Victor's shoulders. 'I don't have to tell you anything,' she replied steadily. 'Will you please get out of here?'

Miguel held her gaze for a few moments longer and then without a word he turned and strode out of the room, slamming all the doors of the house behind him.

After he had gone, Emma breathed a tremulous sigh of relief. She came round Victor's chair to confront him, watching him anxiously as he rubbed his tender muscles.

'Are – are you all right, Victor?'

Victor stretched the muscles tentatively. 'I suppose so,' he replied tersely. Then he swore softly. 'Emma, what was that all about?'

Emma pressed her palms together. 'I – I thought I explained.'

'No.' Victor was very definite about that. 'No, Emma, you did not explain. Your story was that you met him through the agency and he invited you to have supper with him this evening. But, naturally, you refused.'

'Y-yes.'

'His story is somewhat different. As I recall it, there was the question of his taking you out today.'

'And you believe that?'

'Isn't it true?' Victor sniffed. 'Emma, when I came round here today, Mrs. Cook told me you were in bed with a headache. Were you?'

Emma sighed. 'All right – no, I wasn't in bed. I went to Brighton with Miguel Salvaje.'

Victor looked taken aback. 'You did?'

'Yes.' Emma turned away. 'What are you going to do about it?'

'I wish people would stop asking me what I'm going to do about situations they have created,' snapped Victor shortly. 'What do you expect me to do about it?'

Emma shrugged. 'I don't know. Break our engagement, maybe.'

Victor rose from his chair, wincing painfully. 'Is that what you expect me to do?'

'It wouldn't surprise me if you did,' she admitted, turning to look at him again. 'Oh, Victor, I'm sorry. I'm sorry – for everything.'

Victor shook his head. 'So am I. However . . .' He walked slowly over to the cabinet and poured himself a stiff whisky. 'However, I don't particularly want to lose you, Emma. We

– well, we're compatible. We like the same things. And we'll have a good, reliable marriage, I'm sure of it. You're not one of these fly-by-night young women, constantly searching for some new diversion, but you're young, and attractive, and I shall enjoy taking you about with me.'

Emma listened silently, and he went on: 'Your father and I discussed the question of our marriage in detail before he left for Canada, and I am sure he would agree with me that in the circumstances it might be a good idea if we put the date forward.'

'Put the date forward,' echoed Emma faintly.

'Yes. There's no reason why we shouldn't, is there? I think a couple of weeks before Christmas – that's, let me see, four weeks from now – might be a suitable compromise.'

'Four weeks!' Emma was aghast. It was one thing considering the prospect of marriage with Victor in the New Year which was still nebulously distant, and quite another to fix the date only four weeks ahead. 'I – I don't know that I can be ready in that time,' she faltered.

Victor frowned. 'Why not? What is there for you to do? Any couturier in London can supply you with a dress and accessories before then, and if you want bridesmaids, their dresses as well. Just charge it all to me. You might as well. I shall have the responsibility for all your expenditure in future.'

Emma put a hand to her head. 'You're going too fast for me, she said helplessly. 'I – give me a chance to sleep on it, Victor. Good heavens, Daddy might not be back by then.'

'But you said yourself he probably would be. And if we write and tell him about the wedding, he'll have to be, won't he? Perhaps your brother and his wife will come, too.'

Emma shook her head. 'I doubt if they could afford to.'

'Then write and tell them I'll pay their expenses.' Victor was being very generous. 'Emma, my dear, I know I'm not very demonstrative, but I do think a lot of you, I always

75

have, and I want us to be happy.'

'I know you do, Victor.' Emma took a deep breath. 'But it's late – and I do have a headache now, really.'

Victor sobered. 'Oh, yes – Salvaje! I'd almost forgotten about him. I don't know what to do about that.'

'There's nothing to do, is there?' asked Emma tightly.

'I suppose not,' said Victor broodingly, rubbing his muscles ruefully. 'Mind you, I'd like to be able to do something. Coming here – into a person's home – threatening them! Punching me!' He snorted. 'Who the devil does he think he is? And where does he think he is? This is England, you know, not some primitive South American republic where civilization is a dirty word!' He put down his glass and buttoned the jacket of his suit. 'He ought to be taught that you can't behave like that here and get away with it. I've a good mind to have a word with his Embassy—'

'Oh, really, Victor, let it drop,' exclaimed Emma wearily. 'It's over now. Don't stir up any more trouble, because somehow I don't think Mig – Señor Salvaje – cares a great deal for rules and regulations.'

'Then perhaps he should,' retorted Victor pompously. 'Are you defending the man?'

'No, Victor. I'm tired, and I want to go to bed, that's all.'

Victor considered her pale face appraisingly. 'Yes, I must say you do look tired. All right, my dear, I'll go. And don't you go worrying about this Mexican any more. I'll see he doesn't trouble you again.'

Emma wanted to make some comment about that veiled threat, but she was too tired, and in any case, by tomorrow Victor would be so involved with the Messiter deal that he would forget all about what he had said.

The following day, Emma resumed her work at the agency. After a preliminary inquiry about her health, Fenella said nothing more, and Emma decided to let it go at that. After all, Victor would be hardly likely to betray her confidence in the circumstances.

Emma herself felt curiously empty inside, as though all emotion had been drained out of her. She did her work efficiently, but automatically, refusing to allow her mind to dwell on those thoughts it constantly conjured up. Thoughts of the previous day with Miguel, of their companionship, and of those moments on the dunes when he had shown her so effectively how little defence she had against him.

The looming prospect of her marriage to Victor was almost frightening, particularly as she knew that Miguel had been right in one respect at least: she did not love Victor, but whether or not that was because she loved someone else she could not be certain. And nor would she allow herself to speculate in that direction.

On Friday evening they attended the celebratory dinner at the Hansons. It was quite an enjoyable occasion; Emma, naturally, was the youngest person there, but at least it avoided for one evening Victor's increasing demands that she set a date for their wedding and write to her father.

She drank rather a lot of champagne during the course of the evening, and was quite tipsy when Victor drove her home in the early hours of Saturday morning. She was aware of his disapproval, which had dispersed the rather smug air he had been wearing all evening, but she was beyond caring, and although she might regret it at some later date, right now she was enjoying the feeling of release it had given her.

Victor walked up the drive with her to her door, but refused her invitation to come in for coffee. 'It's late,' he said, obviously trying to control his impatience with her. 'I think you'll find you'll feel better if you go straight to bed.'

'I feel fine!' exclaimed Emma brightly.

'Nevertheless, I'm going.' Victor opened the door for her

and then handed her back the key. 'I'll give you a ring later when you're feeling more yourself.'

'Yes, Victor. Of course, Victor.' Emma was provocatively demure.

Victor hesitated, looked as though he would have liked to have said something more and thought the better of it, and then with a brief salute walked quickly away down the drive to his waiting car.

Emma wrinkled her nose at his retreating back, and then pushed wide the door and entered the hall. As she closed the door, however, she noticed a thin thread of light showing beneath the lounge door, and immediately a prickle of apprehension slid along her spine. It could be Mrs. Cook, although she didn't normally stay up so late, or it could be Miguel . . .

But before she had a chance to consider either of these theories, the lounge door was flung open and a strange man confronted her, a man like and yet unlike Miguel Salvaje.

The amount of champagne Emma had consumed cushioned her against any immediate sense of fear or shock at the man's unexpected appearance, and Mrs. Cook appeared hoveringly behind him then, reassuringly wrapped in her warm woollen dressing gown.

The man stood aside, and Mrs. Cook emerged to look uncomfortably at her employer's daughter. 'How late you are!' she said, glancing at the man by her side. 'Er – Señor Castillo has been waiting to speak to you for some time.'

Castillo!

The name rang a bell, and vaguely Emma recalled Miguel's references to his manager. Castillo. Yes, that had been his name.

She stiffened. 'Yes?' she said, with cold, questioning sobriety.

The man gestured into the lounge. 'Please to come and sit down, *señorita*,' he suggested politely.

78

Emma looked at him curiously. The similarities between Señor Castillo and Miguel Salvaje were mostly concerned with their colouring. This man was not so tall as Miguel, but perhaps a little broader, and he was clearly ten or fifteen years older.

'Very well,' she agreed now, and looked at the house-keeper. 'Will you stay with me, Mrs. Cook?'

The man Castillo frowned. 'What I have to say to you is of a confidential nature, *señorita*,' he said. 'As I understand the situation, this good woman is merely your housekeeper, *si*?'

'Mrs. Cook is also my friend,' stated Emma sharply. 'Whatever you have to say – whatever *Señor Salvaje* has sent you to say – can be said in front of her.'

Mrs. Cook moved uncomfortably. 'Now, Miss Emma—' she began.

'Be so good as to leave us, *señora*,' said Castillo bleakly. 'Whatever Miss Seaton says, I insist upon speaking with her privately.'

Emma seethed. 'Might I remind *you*, *señor*, that this is my father's house, and as he is not here I am temporarily the householder. I am not used to being treated as though my feelings were of no account.'

Castillo's mouth drew in. 'I feel I should tell you, *señorita*, that what I have to say is not in your favour, and you may well regret this impulse to confide such matters to a housekeeper!'

Emma's face burned, and Mrs. Cook patted her arm. 'Look, miss,' she murmured, 'I'll just wait in the kitchen. Perhaps you'd like some coffee, hmm?'

Emma moved restlessly. 'Oh, Mrs. Cook,' she exclaimed, but the housekeeper could tell she was weakening.

'As I say,' she said, 'I'll be in the kitchen. If you want me – just call!'

'All right.' Without another word, Emma walked into the

lounge and heard Castillo follow her and close the door. She turned to face him calmly enough, but inside her stomach was churning with sickening rapidity. 'Well?' she demanded coldly. 'What secrets have you to impart?'

'Impart? What is this?' Castillo looked puzzled.

Emma sighed irritably. 'Oh, it means – to tell! Go on, for heaven's sake!'

Castillo considered her for a moment, and then he said: 'Have you seen this?'

He drew a newspaper out of his pocket. It was the evening edition of the *News* and it was folded so that one particular section stood out against all the others. Emma took the paper indifferently enough, but as she read the brief article her hands began to tremble and the words danced meaninglessly before her eyes.

The write-up concerned the Mexican pianist, Miguel Salvaje, who was presently in London to give a series of concerts and recitals. It described how the young pianist had been involved in a brawl after leaving the concert hall late the previous evening and that owing to his injuries the remainder of his tour had had to be cancelled.

Emma looked up in horror. '*Oh, God!*' she breathed, and her cheeks drained of all colour.

Castillo hastily pushed her into a chair and going over to the cabinet poured some brandy into a glass. 'Here!' he said, taking the paper from her nerveless fingers. 'Drink this!'

Emma complied, sipping the fiery liquid hastily, willing the nausea that was enveloping her to go away. She lay back against the soft upholstery, her face pale and drawn. 'Miguel,' she whispered. 'How – how is he? Is he – badly injured?'

Castillo stood before her, legs apart, hands folded behind his back. 'To anyone else, his injuries would be considered minimal,' he replied. 'To Salvaje, they are gigantic.'

'What do you mean?' Emma stared at him.

'He has some facial bruising, a couple of suspected cracked ribs, and several cuts and bruises about his body.'

Emma leant forward. 'Is that all?'

'No. They also broke three of his fingers.'

'Oh, no!' Emma felt a choking sensation in her throat. 'Oh, how terrible!'

'Yes, isn't it?' remarked Castillo pleasantly. 'But rest assured, the culprits will be found and arrested.'

'How – how can you be sure of that?'

'Because – well, because I am sure.' Castillo seated himself in the chair opposite her. 'Now, will you come to see Miguel?'

Emma shrank back. 'Me?'

'Yes, you. He wants to see you.'

Emma finished the brandy and almost choked on it. 'Why – why does he want to see me?'

'I thought for a moment just now that you were concerned about him.'

'I was – I *am*!' Emma bent her head miserably. 'Oh, yes, I am.'

'Then come! My car is not far away.'

'Now?' Emma was astounded.

'But of course. Miguel is still in some pain. He does not sleep much.'

'Of course.' Emma shook her head, her eyes wide. 'But – but how did it happen? I mean – who would want to fight with Miguel?'

Castillo frowned. 'That is not for me to say.'

Emma got up out of her chair, looking down at the long navy crepe dress she was wearing. 'I can't go like this.'

'No.' Castillo inclined his head in assent. 'You will change, *si*?'

Emma nodded, and with a helpless shrug went out of the room.

Immediately upon hearing the door open and close, Mrs.

Cook appeared from the kitchen. 'What's going on?' she whispered.

Emma sighed. 'Miguel's been injured. I – I've got to go and see him.'

'At this hour of the night?' Mrs. Cook looked horrified.

'I know it's late, Mrs. Cook, but I have to go.'

'You're getting involved with that man again, just as everything was settling back to normal,' Mrs. Cook accused her impatiently. 'And what's Mr. Harrison going to say if he finds out about this?'

Emma gestured futilely. 'I don't know. But quite honestly, Mrs. Cook, I don't particularly care – not right now.'

Mrs. Cook shook her head. 'It's not like you to behave like this, Miss Emma. What have you been drinking this evening?'

Emma half smiled. 'Champagne. Do you think that's why I've agreed to go? I can assure you I'm perfectly sober now.'

'And when will you be back?'

'I don't know. Don't wait up, Mrs. Cook.'

Castillo was driving Miguel's Jensen. Sitting beside him as they threaded their way through the quiet streets to the exclusive hotel overlooking Hyde Park where Miguel was staying, Emma couldn't help wishing she had had the time to drink another brandy to bolster her failing confidence. Why did Miguel want to see her after the last time they had parted? What could he possibly have to say to her?

She looked down at her clothes without pleasure. She had hastily pulled on the grey tweed skirt and white blouse she had worn for work that afternoon, and she was aware they gave her a matronly appearance. Still, she thought unhappily, the sheepskin jacket concealed a multitude of sins and no one was likely to ask her to take her coat off, were they?

The night staff at the hotel regarded her curiously as she entered with Castillo, but obviously he was known and they passed without comment. A lift transported them what seemed a tremendous way up the building and they emerged on to a pile-carpeted corridor with vases of exquisite blooms set at intervals between the white panelled doors.

Castillo led the way towards a door at the far end of the corridor and Emma followed him nervously, treading softly for fear of disturbing anyone. Everywhere was silent, and well it might be, she thought, at three-thirty in the morning!

They entered the sumptuously appointed lounge of a suite of rooms, and as Castillo switched on the lamps, Emma looked about her with interest. A soft apricot carpet flowed into every corner, while the comfortable chairs and couches were upholstered in lime green damask. The walls were hung with damask also, hinting at the deeper bronze silk of the curtains. It was a magnificent apartment but dominated by the piano that stood below tall windows, shadowed now by the lighting.

The sight of the instrument brought Emma to the realization that the man she had come to see was not present. 'Where – where is Miguel?'

Castillo lifted her coat from her resisting shoulders. 'One moment, and then I will take you to him.'

Emma made an abortive effort to retain the coat and then gave in. 'But where is he?'

'Here!'

The low voice startled her and she swung round to find Miguel entering the room through one of the inner doors. Dressed only in a purple silk dressing robe, his darkly tanned face paler than she had ever seen it, there was something unbearably attractive and familiar about him, and she had to steel herself not to go to him and throw herself upon his mercy. There were several ugly contusions on his face, and a jagged cut on his cheek that looked painful. But her eyes were drawn to his injured hand, hidden in the pocket of his robe.

Castillo clicked his tongue irritably, going towards the other man and shaking his head reprovingly. 'Miguel! You should not be out of bed! You need to rest. You know that the doctor—'

'*Eso basta!*' Miguel's lips twisted. 'I do not wish to argue with you, Juan. Do you not think Miss Seaton would find an interview in my bedroom too much, even for her?'

Juan Castillo heaved a sigh. 'What Miss Seaton feels is unimportant compared to your health, Miguel. I beg of you—'

Miguel ignored him, looking across the room at Emma. 'Please,' he said politely. 'You will sit down?'

Emma took a few steps towards a low armchair and Juan managed to persuade Miguel to sit down on the couch. Indeed, judging by his pallor Emma thought it unlikely that Miguel had much choice in the matter. She was shocked and unnerved by his appearance and she wished desperately that there was something she could do.

'You will leave us, Juan,' instructed Miguel, with determination.

Juan hesitated, obviously torn between the desire to do what Miguel asked and an equally strong desire to assure himself that nothing untoward would happen in his absence.

'*Juan!*'

There was imperative steel in Miguel's voice now, and with a reluctant sigh the manager left the room.

'Now.' Miguel's dark gaze flickered over Emma. 'Come and sit here.' He indicated the end of the couch.

Emma did as he asked without argument. Miguel was lying on the couch, but it was long enough for there to be plenty of room for her to sit at his feet. This close his

84

bruises were stark and agonizing, and Emma felt the urge to lean forward and put her lips to every inch of his face. Something of what she felt must have shown in her eyes, for Miguel's jaw hardened and he said contemptuously: 'Do not look at me like that. Remember your fiancé! There is to be no more pretence between us!'

Emma was chilled by his words. Folding her hands in her lap, she said quietly: 'Castillo told me about – about your injuries. How did it happen?'

Miguel shrugged. 'It was all over very quickly. We were leaving the theatre after the concert. Juan had gone to get the car, and I was momentarily alone.' He frowned. 'There were three youths, I think. I am not absolutely certain.'

Emma stared at him. 'You mean – they were *waiting* for you?'

'Of course.'

'But I thought – I mean – the papers said it was a – brawl!'

'I suppose it was – although the odds were decidedly uneven.'

'But they implied – oh, you know what I'm trying to say.'

'Yes, I know.'

'But – but why should anyone want to lie in wait for you? To attack you?'

'You don't know?'

Emma stared at him. 'Me? How should I know?'

Miguel ran his uninjured hand down the cut on his cheek. 'Were you out when Castillo came to fetch you? He was a very long time.'

She flushed. 'Yes. Victor and I – that is – we'd been to an anniversary party.'

'An anniversary party!' Miguel considered her hot face dispassionately. 'And how is your inestimable fiancé? Recovered from the nasty shock I gave him the other evening?'

'I expect so.' Emma moved uncomfortably. 'I don't see what this has to do with your injuries.' She sighed. 'I just wish there was something I could do . . .'

'There is.' Miguel smiled, but it was not a pleasant smile. 'That is why I wanted to see you.'

Emma frowned. 'What can I do?'

'You can take a message to your fiancé for me.'

Emma was perplexed. 'A – message? To Victor?'

'That is correct.'

'But what – what message?'

'Just tell him that I know the identity of one of the youths, will you?'

Emma saw the light of cruelty in his eyes and shivered. 'But why should Victor be interested in the identity of these men?'

'Can't you guess?'

Emma rose abruptly to her feet. 'You can't seriously be saying that Victor had anything to do with your injuries!' She stared at him incredulously, a sense of hysteria rising inside her. 'Oh, really, how – how ridiculous!'

'Is it?' Miguel seemed perfectly calm.

'Of course it is. Victor doesn't have any dealings with – with thugs?'

'Did I say they were thugs?'

'No – no, but obviously that's what they were.'

Miguel shrugged indifferently. 'I might have known you would not believe me. Nevertheless, I should be grateful if you would deliver the message.'

'Deliver it yourself!' Emma turned away, breathing fast. She felt hurt and sickened by his words. She didn't know quite what she had expected when she came here, but certainly nothing like this. Trembling a little, she said: 'Will you ask Juan to get my coat? I – I want to go home.'

She did not hear Miguel move, but a few seconds later she felt the warmth of his breath on the back of her neck and realized he was standing just behind her. 'Why do you find it so hard to believe?' he asked softly. 'I've no doubt given the same circumstances I might have done the same thing.'

'I – Victor's not like that!' exclaimed Emma desperately.

'All men are – like that!' he essayed quietly.

Emma's knees were shaking so much she felt sure they must be visible. 'And – and if I give him your message. What – what do you intend to do about it?'

'What do you expect me to do about it?'

'I don't know. Go to the police, I suppose.' She made an involuntary gesture. 'There'll be damages, won't there? As you broke three fingers—'

'*I* did not break three fingers,' he snapped harshly. 'No, Emma, that was not how it happened at all. My fingers were broken deliberately.'

'Oh, no!' Horrified, Emma spun round to face him, a hand pressed to her lips.

'But yes.' Miguel's lips twisted bitterly. 'Would you like to hear how it was done?'

'*No!*' Emma felt physically sick. 'I – oh, please – where's the bathroom?'

Miguel's brows drew together uncomprehendingly, but with a silent gesture he indicated a door to their right. Giving no explanation, Emma sped across the room and dashed into the white and gold luxury of the bathroom, reaching the basin just in time.

When it was all over, she lay against the cool tiled wall weakly. Oh, God, she thought despairingly. That this should be happening to her. She, who had always imagined herself such a calm and well-organized person. All of a sudden the smooth, unruffled cultivation of her life had given way to wild, uncharted wastes, and the agony of it was that in spite of everything it was Miguel Salvaje who filled her mind and senses to the exclusion of everything else . . .

87

CHAPTER SIX

WHEN at last she summoned up enough courage to return to the lounge, she found Juan Castillo bending over a tray of coffee which he had just placed on a low table in the centre of the floor. He straightened at her entrance, but there was no sign of Miguel.

Emma looked round, conscious of a feeling of dishevelment, and put up a nervous hand to her hair. 'Er – where has – he – gone?' she inquired, her voice roughened by what had just occurred.

Juan regarded her intently. 'You are feeling better, *señorita*?'

'I suppose so.' Emma was vague.

'I have persuaded Señor Salvaje to go back to bed,' went on Juan. 'Will you have some coffee before you leave?'

'I couldn't swallow a thing.' Emma shuddered. 'Could I – that is – would it be possible for me to see – Miguel again?'

Juan frowned. 'Again, *señorita*?' He spread his hands expressively. 'I understood your conversation was over.'

Emma twisted her hands together. 'I would like to see him again,' she insisted.

Juan sighed. 'I see.' He looked undecided. 'It's very late, *señorita*.'

'That didn't trouble you earlier when you brought me here,' exclaimed Emma rather heatedly.

Juan hesitated and then he nodded. 'No, that is true. A moment, *señorita*.'

He left her and crossed the room to the door through which Miguel had entered before. The door closed behind him and for a while there was total silence. Emma felt unnerved. The impulse to escape while she had the chance was strong upon her, but something even stronger compelled her to stay.

The inner door opened again and Juan appeared and beckoned her. 'Come! I have told Señor Salvaje you have something further to say to him.'

Emma wondered if that was exactly true. Did she have anything further to say? And if so – what? But she moved automatically towards him, and past him into Miguel's bedroom.

Miguel was not, as she had expected, in bed, but lying on top of it. And it was a very opulent bed with its quilted satin headboard and silken, tasselled covers. The whole room was elaborately furnished, but somehow Emma knew that Miguel would not have chosen such a setting had he had the choice.

Juan waited a moment by the opened door and then with a characteristic shrug went out and closed it behind him. Emma stood uncertainly in the middle of the floor, not quite knowing what to say now.

Miguel took the onus from her however, by saying: 'You are fully recovered, *señorita*?'

Emma nodded. 'I'm sorry.'

'Why be sorry?'

'Well, for – for having to—' She broke off. 'Miguel, I—' She halted and looked miserably down at the thickly carpeted floor.

'Juan tells me that you have something more to say to me,' he urged, but his voice was cool, controlled.

'I – I wanted to ask what you intend to do – about – about the attack.'

'You are concerned for your fiancé, of course,' he remarked bitterly.

'I am concerned – about everything,' she amended, looking at his injured hand, swathed in bandages, lying on the

89

coverlet. 'How – how long will it be before you can – use your fingers again?'

Miguel's jaw tightened. 'Four – maybe six weeks.'

'And your tour is cancelled. You are returning to Mexico.'

'In a few days, yes.'

'Yes.' Emma took a step forward. 'And afterwards – after the fingers mend, how long will it take – I mean, everything will be the same as before, won't it?'

'You mean will I be able to play as well as before, don't you?'

'I suppose I do.'

He shrugged. 'That is in the lap of the gods, as they say. A pianist is an exceptional case. His fingers must be deft, agile, continually in use, continually flexed. If they are not used they begin to stiffen, the muscles harden, they lose their flexibility. To become a successful concert pianist takes years and years of dedication and practice. To anticipate the extent of the damage done by any means except time and experience is impossible.' His eyes narrowed. 'If you came in here seeking reassurance, expecting me to absolve you from all blame, then you will, I am afraid, be disappointed.'

Emma's lips trembled. 'I didn't expect that. On the contrary, I'm overwhelmingly aware that it's all my fault—'

'No.' Miguel swung his legs to the ground and stood up. 'No,' he repeated harshly. 'It is not all your fault. We are all to blame in some measure. But whether the punishment fits the crime is for you to decide.' He walked the few spaces between them and stood looking down at her, his injured hand concealed again in the pocket of his robe. 'You look so guilty, Emma. Why? I do not expect Harrison will lose much more than face.'

Emma glanced up at him. 'You – you still maintain that Victor is involved. How – how can you be so sure?'

'You know a boy called Michael Hanson?'

Emma gasped. 'Of – of course.' Michael Hanson was the nineteen-year-old son of Miles and Delia, at whose anniversary celebrations she had been this evening – with Victor. Unwillingly she recalled Victor's self-satisfied attitude; his smugness which had only been dispersed by her own foolish behaviour. 'Why – why?'

'He was one of the youths that attacked me.'

'*No!*'

'I'm afraid he was.'

'But – but how do you know it was Michael?'

Miguel shrugged. 'He lost something – something that belongs to him.'

'But whatever it is, how – how can you prove you didn't just find it?'

Miguel's expression was wry. 'What a devious little mind you have, Emma. That is a very intelligent observation. However, I am not without friends myself in London, and I think with the evidence at my disposal . . .' He drew out his injured hand and fingered the heavy gold ring inset with a ruby which Emma had noticed before. 'Yes, I think the facial appearance of this boy, Hanson, will take some explaining. I do not consider it will be too difficult to build up a case.'

Nor did Emma. 'And that's what you intend to do?' She licked her lips.

'You have an alternative suggestion?'

'How could I have?' Emma felt sick again. 'I – I'd better go.'

Miguel made no immediate move to prevent her and she moved unhappily towards the door. But then, as she reached for the handle, he said: '*I* have an alternative to offer.'

Emma looked back. 'Yes?'

'Yes.' Miguel folded his arms, his bandaged fingers hidden again. 'Marry me, and come back to Mexico with

91

me, and I will forget all about this – unpleasantness.' His lips twisted. 'At least – I promise not to make things uncomfortable for Harrison.'

Emma grasped the door handle for support. 'What did you say?'

'I think you heard what I said, Emma.' Miguel shrugged. 'Marry me, and the *policia* shall hear no more of this.'

It was too much for her to absorb, and shaking her head a trifle bewildered, she pulled open the door and re-entered the lounge. The room was empty and she stood, swaying a little, her legs like jelly beneath her. She simply could not assimilate what she had just heard.

Miguel followed her and stood leaning against the door jamb watching her as she looked distractedly about for her coat. 'What is wrong?' he queried coldly. 'The suggestion has no appeal, I gather.'

Emma turned to him in confusion. 'I – I don't consider it amusing to be made a fool of,' she said.

'A fool?' He frowned. 'Why should you imagine I am trying to make a fool of you?'

Emma clenched her fists at her sides. 'You can't honestly expect me to believe that you're actually asking me to marry you!'

'Why not?'

Emma's mouth worked helplessly. 'Why should you want to marry me?'

Miguel made an indifferent gesture. 'I have my reasons.'

Emma stared at him, and then sighed in exasperation. 'Oh, honestly!' She lifted a cushion and tossed it down. 'Where's my coat?'

'You're turning me down, then?'

Emma halted again. 'Miguel, this is England! I don't know what outlandish methods you have for choosing a bride out in Mexico, but here there has to be more than just an arrangement!' She sighed again. 'Besides, I don't believe you're really serious, whatever you say.'

'Why?' Miguel came further into the room. 'Why shouldn't I want to marry you?'

Hot tears of frustration sprang to Emma's eyes and she dashed them away with a careless hand. 'Stop it!' she cried, covering her ears. 'I won't listen to any more!'

Miguel came across to her, and when she would have backed away he put his uninjured hand round the back of her neck, gripping it so painfully that she was forced to take a step nearer to him. Her knees brushed the silk hem of his gown and she trembled violently.

'Now,' he said huskily, looking down into her face, 'tell me: why shouldn't I want to marry you?'

Emma swallowed hard. 'Please – let me go, Miguel!'

'No. No, I won't let you go. And you don't really want me to, do you?' He tipped her chin up with his thumb. 'Do you?'

Emma fought for sanity, but she was overpoweringly conscious of his nearness, and when his hand slid down her back propelling her close against him, she realized that only the thin silk of his robe separated her from his lean, muscular body.

With a cry, she tore herself away from him, taking advantage of the fact that he had only one good hand, and not until she looked back at him did she realize that she must have hurt him. The pallor of his face was pronounced and he sought support from the back of a chair.

'Oh, what do you want of me?' she cried.

'I want you,' he replied harshly. 'On my terms.'

She saw what a strain this was placing on him as beads of sweat appeared on his forehead and compassion overcame all else. 'You must go back to bed!' she exclaimed. 'We – we can talk about this when – when you've had time to rest.'

'*No*.' The word was a command. 'I want your answer now

93

'– before you leave this apartment.'

'But I don't know you – anything about you!' she protested.

'You will,' he answered coldly.

'You expect me to break my engagement to Victor and marry you wiithout giving myself time to think?'

'What is there to think?' Miguel's face was hard. 'I wonder what Harrison would say if he knew how you were dicing with his reputation.'

'That's not fair!'

'Nor is this.' Miguel held up his bandaged hand.

'No – no, I know.' Emma sighed. 'But – but I can't make a decision, straight away. I *can't.*'

'Why?'

'Well, because – because it's so – so—'

'Uncivilized?' He uttered a low imprecation. 'Very well, *señorita,* you have twenty-four hours to decide. And I am being more than generous.'

Emma's body sagged. 'I can go now?'

'Yes. You can go.' He turned and walked back into his bedroom, and Emma stared after him helplessly. He had not told her where her coat was, and how was she to get home at – she consulted her watch – five o'clock in the morning!

As Miguel's door had closed behind him, she went nervously over to one of the other doors and knocked. There was no reply, and with great daring she turned the handle. But as the door opened, a sense of hysteria welled up inside her. It was a clothes closet, and there, hanging in front of her, was her coat.

She tugged the coat from its hanger, and put it on, and then started guiltily as another door opened. But it was only Juan Castillo and he looked at her curiously. 'You are going home, *señorita?*'

Emma wondered whether he had expected her to stay. Perhaps he had thought that once in Miguel's bedroom there

94

was little chance that she would emerge before daylight.

'Yes,' she said now. 'Yes, I'm going home.'

'I will take you.'

'That's not necessary. I can get a cab.'

'I insist.' There was the same note of finality in Juan's voice as there had been in Miguel's and Emma gave in gracefully. She was too distraught and tired to make too many objections, and besides, she badly needed to be alone at home to try and make some sense from the confusion of the last hour.

Mrs. Cook was not about when Emma reached home, and yet she sensed somehow that the housekeeper was not asleep. Deciding to make some tea, she was in the kitchen waiting for the kettle to boil when Mrs. Cook came in, rubbing her cheeks tiredly.

'So you're back!' she remarked wearily. 'How is he?'

Emma poured boiling water into the teapot. 'Do you want some tea?'

'Yes, please.' Mrs. Cook looked at her strangely. 'How is Señor Salvaje?'

'He'll survive.' Emma added milk to a second cup. 'How many sugars?'

'Two.' Mrs. Cook perched herself on one of the stools at the breakfast bar. 'How was he injured?'

'Some youths set about him, apparently. As he left the theatre yesterday evening. Or perhaps I should say two evenings ago.' Emma shook her head confusedly. 'There's your tea.'

'Thank you.' Mrs. Cook stirred the steaming liquid absentmindedly. 'That's terrible! Was he badly hurt?'

'Multiple cuts and bruises. But that wasn't the worst of it. They broke three of his fingers.'

'Oh, no!' Mrs. Cook was genuinely shocked. 'How awful!'

'Yes, isn't it?' Emma sipped her tea slowly. But all the time she felt numb. As though none of this was real, not Miguel, or Juan, or even Mrs. Cook, sitting there so re-assuringly, making small talk. It couldn't be real. Victor couldn't have arranged for those boys to attack Miguel, just because the Mexican had given him a few bad moments. And Miguel couldn't have asked her to marry him and leave all this to go to a country she knew nothing about, to live with him God knows where. It was all fantastic; a dream, or perhaps a nightmare; certainly something that would disappear in the light of morning.

'There'll be no more concerts, then,' Mrs. Cook was saying now. 'I suppose they'll catch the culprits, won't they? I mean, it would be terrible if they didn't. There'll be damages, of course. Considering what's at stake, I should think they'd be sky-high, wouldn't you?'

'What?' Emma was absent.

'The damages! Heavens! Pianists' fingers are insured for thousands of pounds, you know.' She touched Emma's arm. 'Aren't they?'

Emma sighed. 'Oh, yes, I suppose so.'

'You don't sound very concerned,' remarked Mrs. Cook dryly. 'Well, whoever is responsible deserves all they get, that's all I can say. They may have ruined his career, not to mention his life.' She shook her head. 'The violence that goes on in London today frightens me, it really does! Young thugs! They want a few strokes of the cat, that would settle them down!'

'Oh, stop it, can't you?' Emma's nerves were frayed to breaking point, and she couldn't prevent the outburst.

Mrs. Cook stared at her in surprise. 'Well, I'm sorry, I'm sure,' she said huffily, but Emma shook her head and gripped the older woman's arm tightly.

'No! No, don't get upset, Mrs. Cook. I – I couldn't bear that. Not right now.'

Mrs. Cook frowned. 'What is it? What's the matter with you? Why are you looking like that?' An expression of dawning comprehension came over her face. 'That man – he – he hasn't—'

Emma made an impatient gesture. 'No, no, no! He's not seduced me, if that's what you're thinking. Nothing like that.'

'Then what is wrong?'

Emma traced the pattern of the wood grain with a careless finger. 'Lots of things,' she answered distractedly.

Mrs. Cook sniffed. 'Oh, Miss Emma! As soon as you get involved with that man again there's trouble! For heaven's sake, have nothing more to do with him!'

Emma gave a mirthless laugh, and Mrs. Cook looked really concerned. 'You're tired,' she said reprovingly. 'You get along upstairs to bed, and if Mr. Harrison comes round this morning I'll tell him you can't see him.'

Emma gave the housekeeper a faint smile. 'Oh, Mrs. Cook, if only it was that simple.'

'What do you mean?'

'What I say.' Emma realized that no matter how she might pretend otherwise it was real, everything was real, and that sooner or later Mrs. Cook would have to learn the truth. Taking a deep breath, she said: 'He wants me to marry him.'

Mrs. Cook could not have looked more astounded. 'Who? This – this Salvaje fellow?'

'That's right.' Emma returned her attention to her tracing. 'He asked me – about half an hour ago.'

Mrs. Cook gasped and got up to get herself another cup of tea. 'I – I can't believe it,' she exclaimed. 'Why, he hardly knows you.'

'I don't know him at all,' replied Emma flatly.

'Oh, it's ridiculous!' Mrs. Cook came back to her seat. 'Isn't it?'

'Is it?'

'Well, don't you think so?' Mrs. Cook frowned. 'You haven't – well – accepted him, have you?'

'No.' Emma was abrupt.

'Thank the Lord for that!' Mrs. Cook raised her eyes heavenward. Then she looked again at Emma, 'So what's all this about?'

'I haven't – *refused him* – either.'

'What? But what about Mr. Harrison?'

'Indeed! What about Mr. Harrison?' Emma was sarcastic.

'You know you're going to marry Mr. Harrison,' went on Mrs. Cook severely. 'Good heavens, you're just talking nonsense! You love Mr. Harrison and he loves you. I think he's been very patient with you in the circumstances.'

'Do you?' Emma sounded cynical. 'I'm fond of Victor, of course . . .' But even as she said the words a mental image of Miguel's bandaged fingers rose before her eyes. The Victor she was fond of would never have arranged such a brutal assault. Perhaps she didn't know him at all. They said you didn't know a man until you lived with him . . .

Mrs. Cook tapped her fingers on the table top nervously. 'I think you're just saying all this to upset me,' she said. 'You can't seriously be considering marrying this – this – *foreigner*!'

Emma sighed. 'Don't you like him?'

Mrs. Cook snorted. 'I've only met the man a couple of times, and on neither of those occasions did he behave in a way I would have approved of.'

'Why? Because he didn't adhere to the rules?'

'Rules? What rules?' Mrs. Cook was confused.

Emma shook her head. 'Never mind,' she replied. A sense of inevitability was overtaking her and she could have smiled to herself when she considered how complacently she had gone out to the Hansons' party with Victor, never dreaming that within twelve hours her whole life would have been turned upside down.

Mrs. Cook rose to her feet. 'Well, if you're going to talk like this I'm going back to bed. I don't know what's got into you, Miss Emma! I've said it before, and I'll say it again, this man causes nothing but trouble, and you're a fool if you have anything more to do with him.'

Emma looked up at her. 'Lots of girls would envy me,' she remarked dryly. 'He's a very attractive man, don't you think so?'

Mrs. Cook pursed her lips reprovingly. 'It's nothing to do with me,' she said shortly. 'But I think you'd better write to your father and ask his opinion before you decide to do anything rash.'

'I couldn't do that,' Emma returned her attention to her half empty cup. 'I have to give him an answer this evening.'

Mrs. Cook caught her breath, and then turning, walked determinedly out of the kitchen.

After she had gone, Emma hunched her shoulders and propped her chin on her fists. If only her father had been there, she thought longingly. But then, if he had, she could never have told him the truth any more than she could tell Mrs. Cook.

But there was one person who she could tell, and that was Victor. He *should* know. And besides, she wanted to see his face when she confronted him with Miguel's accusation.

There seemed no point in going to bed. She knew her mind would not let her rest. Besides, she had things to do.

She bathed and dressed in a blue woollen dress with a white collar and cuffs which together with her coronet of braids gave her a nunlike appearance, and then went downstairs in search of Mrs. Cook. She knew the housekeeper was up and about, and when she entered the lounge she found her there cleaning out the grate.

'Are you wanting breakfast?' Mrs. Cook was chillingly polite.

'Nothing, thanks.' Emma hesitated. 'I'm going out for a while. If Mr. Harrison phones, will you ask him to come round about twelve?'

'Very good, miss.'

Emma sighed, but it was obvious that for the moment Mrs. Cook was unapproachable. With a shrug, she went out again, and after collecting her coat and her handbag left the house.

She drove into the West End, and parked the Mini with difficulty. It was Saturday morning and although it was barely nine o'clock the streets were busy. She found the salon she was looking for in a side street off Oxford Circus. One of the girls at the agency had once mentioned it as being very select and very exclusive, and that was what she wanted.

It was one of those establishments that cater for every detail of a woman's appearance, from hair-styling to foot manicures. Emma had never been in such a place before, and she felt terribly self-conscious as she approached the reception desk.

But when she left the salon less than two hours later, she knew she looked a different person. She had allowed the assistant to choose what make-up she needed, but she had made some small contribution towards choosing a hair-style. She had had her hair cut so that now it was only a little longer than shoulder length, and the ends turned gently inward. Freed from confinement, the rich amber colour was not subdued, and it curved over her shoulders and under her chin with confiding silkiness. She would never have believed changing her hair-style could make such a sweeping change in her appearance, and even the plain blue puritan dress had lost its severity. The natural creamy quality of her skin had been accentuated by the clever use of cosmetics, and a pale green eye-shadow gave her eyes a faintly oriental slant. A sliver of excitement slid down her spine when she considered Miguel's reactions to what she had done, but she squashed it instantly. She had not done this for Miguel's benefit, she told herself fiercely, but to prove to Victor that she was not the mouse he thought she was.

She was making her way back to where the Mini was parked when a slack suit in a boutique window caught her eye. It was made of a dark blue jersey cloth, the slacks flared, the jacket fitting.

On impulse she entered the shop and when she came out half an hour later she was wearing the suit. Together with her new hair-style and make-up, she looked young and modern, and very attractive, and she was conscious that several pairs of male eyes turned in her direction as she walked along Oxford Street. It was an intoxicating experience for someone who had constantly avoided the limelight, and by the time she reached the Mini she was flushed and unaccountably exhilarated.

She arrived back at the house just before noon to find Victor's saloon outside. Immediately, her new-found confidence fled, and a palpitating apprehension filled her being.

Victor was in the lounge, drinking the coffee Mrs. Cook had provided for him, and looked up welcomingly when she opened the door. But then his mouth dropped open and he stared at her as though he had never seen her before. His cup clattered into its saucer and he rose to his feet, frowning.

'Whatever have you been doing?' he demanded roughly. 'My God, Emma, what do you think you look like?'

Emma glanced at her reflection in the wall mirror and was satisfied with what she saw. 'I've had my hair cut,' she announced calmly. 'Do you like this suit? It's new.'

'I can see it is.' Victor was grim. 'I don't know what all

this is in aid of, Emma, but—'

'Oh, stop blustering, Victor!' she exclaimed. 'All I've done is have my hair cut, after all.'

'You look – different.'

'You mean younger,' remarked Emma dryly. 'Can I have some coffee? I'm feeling rather in need of sustenance. I've been out since eight-thirty.'

'So Mrs. Cook told me.' Victor was still glowering. 'Where have you been?'

'To the hairdressers',' replied Emma, pouring herself a cup of coffee. 'Did you ring?'

'Yes. About eleven. I didn't think you'd be awake before then.'

'I didn't go to bed.' Emma turned, stirring her cup and saw Victor's face getting more and more frustrated.

'Why not?' he asked harshly.

'Because after you had gone last night, I went out.'

'You *went out*?' Victor clenched his fists. 'Are you trying to tell me something, Emma?'

'How did you guess?' Emma would never have believed she could be so much in command of the situation. Bending her head, she went on: 'I went to see Miguel.'

She heard Victor's swift intake of breath. 'What did you say?'

'You heard me, Victor. I said I went to see Miguel—'

'I know what you said,' Victor seethed. 'Get to the point!'

'You know, of course, that he has had to cancel his concert tour?' She was watching him closely now.

Victor hesitated. Obviously he was torn between appearing to have too much knowledge or too little. 'I – er – I believe I did read something of the sort. What of it?'

'Do you know why he has had to cancel his tour?'

Victor moved restlessly. 'Yes. There was some kind of a brawl outside the concert hall, wasn't there?'

'That's right. Only it wasn't a brawl, Victor. Some youths deliberately beat him up.'

Victor's lip curled. 'So what? No doubt he deserved it, filthy foreigner!'

Emma stared at him as if she had never seen him before. 'You can't be serious!'

Victor shrugged. 'What do you expect? I can't feel sympathy for the fellow. Not after what happened the other night.'

Emma put down her coffee cup. 'That rankled, didn't it?'

Victor's eyes narrowed. 'What the hell do you mean by that? Of course it rankled, as you put it. If you ask me, he's got nothing more than he deserved!'

Emma was trembling now, but she had to go on. 'You mean you would condone that kind of brutality, given the right circumstances?'

Victor ran a finger round the inside of his collar. 'I didn't say that. You're just twisting my words to take some of the onus off yourself. You still haven't told me why you went to see him. Or am I supposed to let that go?'

'Oh, no! I wouldn't have told you if I hadn't wanted you to know!'

'Why, you—' He bit off an epithet, and then seemed to realize that they were having their first real argument. 'Look, Emma, let's start at the beginning, shall we? Why did you go to see Salvaje?'

'Because he sent for me.'

'He *sent* for you? What's that supposed to mean? Has the fellow got some hold over you, because, by God, if he has, I'll—'

'You'll what, Victor? Arrange another – *brawl*? Get one or two of your business associates' sons to pretend they're thugs.' She hesitated. 'Like Michael Hanson, for example?'

CHAPTER SEVEN

VICTOR'S face turned purple, and became so mottled that Emma thought at first he was ill. But then he found his voice, and ground out angrily: 'What the hell are you implying?'

Emma sighed, unwilling to go on suddenly. The joy had gone out of it. It had become cruel and sordid. She had seen all she needed to see in Victor's face.

'It's true, isn't it?' she said quietly. 'You did do that, didn't you?'

Victor blustered, 'I don't know what you're talking about. Just because the fellow treated me abominably, you think I'd take the trouble to arrange to have him beaten up—'

Emma turned away. 'Michael lost something,' she said dully. 'Something that identifies him.'

There was silence for a moment, and then he went on again: 'If this is some kind of joke, Emma, I think it's in very bad taste.'

'So do I,' said Emma, with a weary gesture. 'Don't bother to go on, Victor. I know, I tell you, I know!'

Victor was breathing noisily, striding restlessly about the room, muttering to himself. 'Never heard of such a thing,' he snapped. 'Accusing *me*! If Hanson was involved, it's nothing to do with me!'

Emma turned on him. 'All right, all right. If you weren't involved you have nothing to fear, have you?'

'What do you mean?'

'I mean that when Miguel puts it into the hands of the police, your name won't be involved.'

Victor halted, his expression grim. 'You're telling me that Salvaje has evidence which convicts Michael?'

'That's right.'

'He told you this?'

'Yes.'

'That was why he sent for you?'

'Yes.'

'I see.' Victor chewed at his lower lip savagely. 'Bloody young fool!' he muttered. 'As if he hadn't the sense to leave all incriminating belongings at home!'

'I presume you mean Michael?'

Victor considered her for a long moment and then seemed to come to a decision. 'All right, all right,' he admitted reluctantly. 'I was involved. But it wasn't supposed to happen the way it did.'

'What's that supposed to mean?' Emma felt a sense of distaste just looking at him.

Victor hunched his shoulders. 'Well, it wasn't meant to turn out so – seriously. Good God, Emma, I'm not some petty criminal arranging a mugging! It was all pretty ridiculous really. I was in the club a couple of nights ago with Hanson, Miles Hanson, and Bob Verity, and I'd had a few drinks – you know how it is. Well, I suppose I just let out the fact that this man Salvaje had been bothering you . . .'

'Oh, God!' Emma stared at him contemptuously.

'Well, it was true, wasn't it?' Victor looked momentarily truculent. Then he went on: 'Anyway, they agreed with me. These foreigners shouldn't be allowed to come over here bothering our women!' His voice gathered strength, as though by re-telling what had happened he was finding excuses for his guilt. 'Of course, when they said he deserved to be taught a lesson I agreed with them, but it didn't quite turn out like that.'

'No.' Emma bent her head. 'I suppose you just hoped to discredit him, to make it appear he indulged in brawls!'

'That's right.' Victor sounded eager. 'That's right. How was I to know the fellow would retaliate? He brought it all upon himself. They'd never have stood on his fingers—'

'Oh, stop it, stop it!' Emma was horrified. 'Do you think because you didn't intend them to get so rough that you're exonerated from what happened? My God, Victor, you may have destroyed that man's career!'

'Oh, rubbish!' Victor mumbled sheepishly. 'Fingers mend—'

'Yes, but in the meantime, what then? He can't practise, his muscles will stiffen. They may never be so flexible again.'

'You're dramatizing the whole thing!' Victor declared hotly. 'Well, let him go to the police, that's what I say. We'll see who has friends around here.'

'Victor, stop it!' Emma had heard enough. Fumblingly, she drew off her diamond engagement ring. 'Here! Take this! We're finished!'

Victor was obviously astounded. 'Now look here, Emma—'

'No, you look here!' she interrupted sharply. 'I thought I knew you – I thought I knew everything about you. But I don't. All right, Miguel shouldn't have hit you the other evening, but if he hadn't you were quite prepared to use any methods to throw him out of the house.'

'And why not?'

Emma shook her head. 'All right, maybe I'm to blame. After all, if I hadn't got involved with him, none of this would have happened.'

'I wondered when you'd realize that!' snorted Victor resentfully. 'Making a fool of yourself! I suppose that's why you've changed your hair-style – bought those ridiculous teenage clothes—'

'They're not teenage clothes. And I bought them because I wanted to prove something to myself. As for making a fool of myself, I don't see how.'

Victor sneered, 'Don't you? You don't suppose I'm in any

doubt as to why you've broken our engagement, do you? You think that if you're free, Salvaje might become interested in you. Well, I shouldn't count on it! From what I hear, you're not the only pebble on his beach—'

Emma's face burned. 'I'd like you to go, Victor.'

'And if I don't want to?'

Emma looked round helplessly. She could hardly see Mrs. Cook rushing to her aid in the circumstances.

'Please,' she said. 'We have nothing more to say to one another.'

'I disagree.' Victor was breathing heavily, rivulets of perspiration running down his forehead. 'Emma, be sensible—'

Suddenly the door bell rang. And as on that other occasion when Miguel had arrived so unexpectedly, Emma and Victor stood motionless, waiting for Mrs. Cook to answer the door.

'If that's Salvaje, I'll break his bloody neck!' muttered Victor furiously, but the veins that stood out on his thick neck bore witness to his extreme state of tension.

The lounge door opened and Mrs. Cook appeared. 'It's Señor Castillo, miss,' she said expressionlessly.

Emma drew a shaky breath. 'Oh! Well, show him in, Mrs. Cook, will you?'

Victor frowned angrily. 'Castillo!' he muttered. 'Who the devil's he?'

Emma ignored him and went forward as Juan Castillo entered the room, dark, and broad, and somehow familiar in his navy overcoat and dark suit. The Mexican's gaze flickered over Victor speculatively, and then he gave his attention to Emma, his eyes mirroring his admiration.

'*Buenos dias, señorita.*'

Emma smiled nervously. 'H-hello. Er – this is – Mr. Harrison; Victor, this is Señor Salvaje's manager, Señor Castillo.'

The two men nodded at one another. Victor made no attempt to shake hands and the Mexican's lips curled faintly. Emma felt awkward. What was she supposed to do now?

However, Juan seemed to have no such inhibitions. 'Miguel sent me,' he explained, focusing his attention on Emma. 'He thought there might be some questions you would like to ask that I could answer.'

'Oh! Oh, I see.' Emma glanced helplessly at Victor. Then she indicated an armchair and looking at Juan said: 'Won't you sit down?'

Juan unfastened his overcoat, but he didn't sit down and Emma sighed. 'Er– Mr. Harrison was just leaving,' she ventured at last.

'Oh, was he?' Juan raised his dark eyebrows questioningly. Then he stepped backward and opened the door again. 'Permit me!'

Victor's jaw tightened and for an instant Emma thought he was about to say something more, but then common sense seemed to assert itself and instead he looked at Emma, weighing the ring she had returned to him in his hand. 'We'll talk later,' he said insistently.

Emma held up her head. 'I don't think so, Victor.'

Victor hesitated, thrust the ring into his jacket pocket, and then walked out of the room. When Emma would have followed to see him out, Juan closed the door between them, and she halted uncertainly.

'You have made your decision, *señorita*?'

Emma looked at him, and shrugged slowly. 'I – oh, yes, I suppose so.'

Juan nodded. 'Is good,' he said, with satisfaction, and took off his overcoat.

Emma gathered her composure. 'Can I offer you a drink?'

'Coffee, perhaps,' replied Juan. 'I do not drink anything

but *tequila,* and I somehow do not think you have any of that, have you?'

Emma shook her head. 'I – er – I'll just ask Mrs. Cook to make some coffee.'

Juan inclined his head politely, and with another shrug she gathered together the cups she and Victor had used on to the tray and carried them out. Mrs. Cook was still uncommunicative, but Emma merely requested the coffee and left her. She had no intention of indulging in another argument with the housekeeper right now.

Juan was an easy companion. He drank his coffee and talked casually about the contrasts between his country and hers, making her laugh as he described his first encounter with the colder climate of North America. Then, as she relaxed with him, he said: 'You want to know about Miguel, *si?'*

Emma flushed. 'You make it sound so – so inquisitive.'

'But no.' Juan shook his head. 'In my country where marriages can still be arranged by parents when their children are but babes in arms, it is common for arrangements to be discussed by representatives of both parties. However, in your case, your father is away, is he not?'

Her father!

Emma shifted restlessly. What would he really say to all this? When he discovered she had broken her engagement with Victor? She could almost hear the dissension in his voice. He had always liked Victor, they had a lot in common, but that didn't mean she had to marry him, she told herself desperately. But what would he think of Miguel? a small voice answered. A musician; a moody alien individual; a South American!

Juan was watching her expressive face, and with perception he said: 'You do not think your father will approve if you go ahead with this, do you?'

'You – you know – about – about—'

'I know Miguel has asked you to marry him, yes.'

'Do – do you approve?' Emma leant towards him.

Juan considered her thoughtfully. 'I don't know. I don't know you well enough to be able to answer that.'

'And I don't know Miguel either!' she exclaimed.

'That is why I am here,' observed Juan quietly.

'All right, tell me about him. How old is he? Where does he live? Does he have any family?'

Juan drew a cheroot out of his pocket and asked whether she objected. Emma shook her head and after lighting it, he said: '*Bien*, I will try to explain. Miguel lives with his father at Lacustre Largo – that is the name of his father's house, you understand.' Emma nodded and he went on: 'It is a beautiful place, a beautiful part of the country!' He pressed his thumb and forefinger together with obvious pride. 'So! His father is a rich man, a very rich man, with much land and much resources.' He considered the glowing tip of his cheroot. 'Always, Don Carlos is keen that Miguel should become a concert pianist! He was always – how do you say it – er—'

'Adept?' supplied Emma questioningly.

'*Si*, that will do. He was adept at playing the piano. From being a very little boy, you understand.' Emma nodded again and Juan smiled. 'So – when he is older, he is successful, very successful, and Don Carlos is delighted!'

'You haven't mentioned Miguel's mother. Is she dead? Doesn't he have any brothers or sisters?'

Juan hesitated, and then at last he said: '*Si, señorita*, Miguel has brothers and sisters. His mother lives, also.'

'Oh!' Emma felt slightly relieved. There was something reassuring about a mother – brothers and sisters.

'Miguel will tell you about his family himself,' Juan was saying now. 'Is there anything else?'

'You haven't told me how old he is.'

'Thirty-three, *señorita*,' Juan smiled. 'Is that all?'

Emma cupped her chin on her hand. 'No. There are heaps of queries, but they will have to wait.' She rose abruptly to her feet. 'Mine is not an easy decision, *señor*.'

She turned to him. 'You haven't told me how he is this morning.'

'Better, I think. At least the ribs are easier. He slept after you had gone, and that is what he needs – rest! He will get it at Lacustre Largo.'

Emma stared at him. 'He's going home? When?'

'The end of next week, I believe, *señorita*.'

'The end of next week?' Emma was astounded. 'And I suppose if I – if I agree to marry him – he will come back after Christmas.'

Juan frowned. 'After Christmas, *señorita*? No. If you are to marry Miguel, you will leave when he does.'

Emma gasped, 'But I couldn't! I mean – I should have to write to my father . . . in Canada. He would want to be here—'

Juan rose now, looking at her patiently. 'That is impossible, *señorita*.'

Emma made a helpless movement of her hands. 'But you can't mean to tell me that Miguel expects me to marry him before we leave?'

'That is exactly his intention, *señorita*,' replied Juan calmly. 'And what is more, I think you will do it!'

Emma went to see Miguel that evening. She had taken some time deciding what to wear and had finally put on one of the dresses Victor had liked so much. It was very plain, its navy darkness unrelieved by any adornment, and yet with her newly styled hair it looked altogether different. She had been tempted to keep on the trouser suit, but it was hardly the attire for an evening appointment, and besides, she was no longer trying to prove anything – to anyone.

To her surprise, a girl let her into the suite, a tall, dark girl dressed in a long black skirt and a white frilled blouse. She was a very attractive young woman and Emma felt the first twinges of something she was later to recognize as jealousy.

'Good evening, *señorita*.' The girl was polite but cool. 'Please to come in. Señor Salvaje will be with you in a few moments.'

She took Emma's black cape and hung it away and then crossed to a small bar and offered her a drink. Emma chose sherry, and a few moments later the glass was put into her hand.

'Please to sit down,' said the girl, taking charge of the situation. 'You are Señorita Seaton, of course. My name is Loren Delmar. I am secretary to Señor Salvaje.'

Miguel's secretary! Emma was surprised. She had not known he possessed the services of a secretary. But then she knew very little about his entourage at all. There was no sign of Juan Castillo this evening and she was rather disappointed. She had felt at ease with the quiet, older man. Perhaps it was a legacy from Victor and her father, she thought. She was used to older men.

'You have a job, *señorita*?' Loren was asking now, and Emma dragged her attention back to the present.

'I – yes. I'm a sort of secretary, too, I work in an agency.'

'I see.' Loren looked politely interested. 'You live in London?'

'Kensington,' Emma nodded.

There was silence for a few moments as they both tried to think of something else to say, and then someone knocked at the outer door. Loren sprang to her feet.

'Ah! That will be Paul,' she said, with a faint smile. 'Excuse me a moment.'

She went to the door and opened it, and glancing round Emma saw another man entering the suite. He was about the same height as Juan, but fairer, with silvery blond hair that fell over his forehead. Emma hadn't the faintest idea who he might be, so she remained where she was and tried to quell the butterflies which were beginning to disturb her stomach.

Loren brought the newcomer across to the chair where Emma was sitting and said: 'Allow me to present Señor Paul Gregory, *señorita*. Paul, this is – Señorita Seaton.'

'Doesn't she have a name?' queried Paul Gregory, with a smile, and Emma took an immediate liking to him. She recalled his name, too. Miguel had been coming from Paul Gregory's house the night he had given her a lift in the fog.

'Yes,' she said now, as he took her hand in greeting. 'I'm Emma.'

'Emma!' He said the name slowly. 'Yes, I like it.' He turned back to Loren. 'Get me a Scotch, there's a good girl. I'm parched. The city traffic is appalling at this hour of the evening.'

Loren Delmar twisted her lips, and then with an indifferent shrug went to do his bidding, but Emma sensed she didn't care for the casual dismissal. Paul Gregory didn't seem to notice, however, and subsided into the chair nearest to her and said: 'Isn't it terrible about Miguel's fingers?'

Emma gripped the stem of her glass so tightly she was amazed it didn't snap. 'Yes,' she managed tautly. 'Terrible!'

'How long have you two known one another?'

Emma was at a loss for words. Until that moment, they had been strangers, meeting for the first time, with no strings attached. But suddenly, by his question, he had placed her in a certain position, and she wasn't sure how to answer him.

But she didn't have to answer him. Miguel's door opened and Miguel himself came into the room, dark and attractive in a dark grey lounge suit and matching waistcoat. His linen was immaculately white, his tie subdued and faultless, and Emma's heart turned over painfully.

Paul rose and went to meet him, exchanging a few low words with him in private before saying conversationally: 'I was just asking Emma how you two met.'

Miguel's gaze flickered towards Emma, still seated in her chair, and the look he gave her was almost insolently appraising. The bruises on his face were less pronounced this evening, and his face had lost the sallow pallor it had possessed in the early hours of the morning. Only his bandaged hand looked exactly as before.

Deciding, as everyone else was standing, she should stand also, Emma, stood up, and as she did so, Miguel said: 'We met one foggy night about three weeks ago. Didn't we – Emma?'

Emma nodded. 'I – suppose it was about three weeks ago,' she agreed. 'How – how are you feeling?'

'I'm fine.' Miguel smiled faintly, his teeth white and even. 'And you?'

'Fine.' Emma felt rather self-conscious, aware of Loren's curious stare.

'Good.' Miguel seemed totally unaware of her tension. 'I've ordered dinner to be sent up in half an hour. Does that suit everyone?'

Paul rubbed his stomach. 'Indeed it does. I don't mind admitting I'm starving.'

'You were parched when you arrived,' remarked Loren dryly.

'So I was. Well, isn't that the way to come to a dinner party? Ready and willing to enjoy the host's hospitality?'

Everyone smiled at this, and Emma tried to relax. But this wasn't at all the scene she had envisaged. She had expected to see Miguel alone and give him her answer, not to join this private dinner party.

Talk became general and as Emma was not near enough

to Miguel to speak privately to him, she was forced to behave as though she had expected all this. Dinner was served on the polished table in the corner of the lounge, served by waiters from the heated trolley they had brought. It was a delicious meal, but as on that other occasion when Emma had had lunch with Miguel, she found her appetite sadly lacking. However, she managed to eat the prawn cocktail and a little fish before tackling the roast duckling. There was a strawberry gateau for dessert and this even she could not resist, finding Miguel's eyes upon her as she finished the last morsel of cream in her dish and wiped her mouth on a table napkin.

Embarrassed at the intensity of that gaze, she immediately turned to Paul and made some inane comment about the luxury of having strawberries in November, hoping that when next she looked across the table Miguel would have found something different to occupy him.

The meal over, the table was cleared and the trolley taken away, and coffee was served on the low table near the comfortable couch and armchairs. Emma was about to take one of the armchairs when she found Miguel's fingers round her wrist, and he drew her deliberately to the couch and seated himself beside her. He did not release her wrist even after they were seated, and Emma was conscious that both Loren and Paul had noticed the intimacy of that little gesture.

The evening passed away pleasantly enough, although Emma found it hard to concentrate on anything but Miguel. When he spoke she listened and when he was not speaking she found her eyes drawn to his lean dark features. Once, when he was saying something to Paul, he found her eyes upon him and he returned that gaze, continuing to talk to Paul as though nothing had happened. But something had happened to Emma, and she was forced to look away. Her breathing was constricted, and a trembling awareness of her

115

need of him was invading her lower limbs. She *needed* him. She knew that now. But was that love? Was this aching agony for possession only infatuation? Was she allowing his undoubted physical magnetism to blind her to what might otherwise have been recognizable? She didn't know. But she did know one thing: she *would* marry him!

At eleven o'clock, Paul finally said he would have to go. Rising to his feet, he looked down at Emma and said: 'Can I give you a lift?'

Emma was about to agree when Miguel stood up too, and shook his head. 'Thank you, Paul, but I shall see that Emma gets home safely.'

Paul gave him a wry look. 'Of course, of course. That was rather *de trop*, wasn't it? Okay, Miguel. I'll ring you next week.'

'Fine.' Miguel grinned warmly at the other man and Paul held his hand firmly for a long moment. Then with a nod, he walked towards the door, and raising his hand in salute let himself out.

Immediately, Miguel turned to the other girl. 'I'd like to speak to Emma alone, Loren,' he said. 'Do you mind?'

Loren shrugged. 'Of course not, Miguel. I will go to bed.' She looked at Emma. 'Good night, *señorita*.'

'Her name is Emma,' remarked Miguel quietly.

'Very well. Good night, Emma.' Loren inclined her head.

'Good night — Loren.' Emma managed a smile, and watched the Mexican girl walk elegantly across the room to disappear into one of the other rooms of the suite.

Once Loren had gone, Miguel moved and put some distance between them, deliberately, Emma thought uneasily. Unable to prevent herself, she said: 'Does — does Loren sleep here? In your suite?'

Miguel looked up from lighting one of the long thin cigars he favoured. 'Yes,' he agreed formally.

Emma twisted her hands together. 'But isn't it – I mean – don't you think that's rather unusual?'

Miguel gave her a wry look. 'If you mean do I sleep with her, why don't you say so?'

Emma coloured hotly. 'It's none of my business.'

'Isn't it?' Miguel put his cigar between his teeth.

'Well, do you, then?' she demanded tremulously.

'No.'

Emma bent her head. 'But – have you?'

'In the past, you mean? No.'

Emma looked up. 'But why does she sleep here? In your suite?'

'Because it's convenient that she should. Juan sleeps here also. A suite of rooms with several bedrooms is very little different from a house, you know.'

'I suppose not.' Emma moved uncomfortably.

'Well?' Miguel took the cigar out of his mouth again. 'Have you come to a decision?'

'Well – yes and no.' Emma sighed. 'I'll marry you – but I can't come to Mexico with you straight away.'

'Why not?' His voice was hard.

'Well, for one thing, there's my father to consider.'

'Where is he?'

'In Canada, with my brother and his wife.'

'Canada?' Miguel stared at her. 'You cannot mean to tell me that you expect me to wait while you write to your father for his approval?'

'Something like that,' murmured Emma uneasily.

'No!' He was adamant.

'What do you mean – no?'

'What I say.' He put his hand into his inside pocket and drew out some papers. 'See! Do you know what this is? It is a marriage licence, made out in our two names. And this – this is a permit supplied by my own consul here in London. I have made inquiries, and we can be married next Thursday.' He spread a hand expressively. 'Once you are my wife, all difficulties concerning immigration are made simple, and naturally you will have the right to Mexican citizenship.'

Emma put a hand to her forehead. 'You – you're going too fast for me,' she murmured faintly. 'How – how can you have these papers? You don't even know whether I'm going to agree to marry you yet.'

Miguel regarded her intently. 'Very well, then. What is your answer?'

Emma moved her head helplessly. 'I – I suppose it's yes. But really, Miguel, I can't—'

'*Eso basta!* That is enough. If this problem of your father troubles you so, we will return to Mexico by way of Montreal and you may go and see him for yourself.'

Emma swayed a little. 'Go – to Canada!' she echoed.

'Why not? It will not be so far out of our way, and besides, I should meet your father. Emma, when you marry me, you will become a rich woman. Surely that must mean something, even to you.'

His tone was sardonic and she wondered exactly what he was thinking. It had all begun to sound unreal again, and even Victor's sordid involvement with those youths seemed less fantastic than what Miguel was suggesting now.

'And – and if I refuse?' she murmured.

Miguel's jaw tightened, and a trace of that ruthlessness she had seen before flickered across his face. 'I do not think you will,' he replied grimly, and she wondered if anyone had ever been allowed to thwart his plans . . .

CHAPTER EIGHT

THE cry of a mountain lion disturbed the stillness of the night and Emma sat bolt upright in the huge bed, wrapping her arms about her chiffon-clad body in alarm. How close it had sounded. How near to the house did animals come? Had they ever invaded the grounds of the estate?

She looked towards the terrace beyond the floor-length windows of her room, but there was nothing to be seen. Moonlight spilled its paleness over mosaic tiling and basket-woven chairs, and beyond the terrace the tropical brilliance of plant life was unnaturally robbed of its colour.

Trembling, she lay down again and tried to sleep. But it was useless. She felt lost and utterly alone, and she rolled on to her stomach trying to tell herself that it was silly feeling this way when she was a married woman now and her husband was only a few yards away in the adjoining room.

But that was the whole crux of the matter, she thought despairingly, feeling hot tears burning at the backs of her eyes. She had thought she knew why Miguel wanted to marry her; she had vainly imagined that it was a combination of mutual attraction and his desire to take her away from Victor, but it seemed now that it had been neither of those things. Since the night she had visited his suite at the London hotel and accepted his proposal of marriage, he had never even touched her, and she didn't know how much longer she could bear it.

She supposed she was painfully naïve when it came to understanding men. She had had so little experience, after all. And this evening, after their stormy arrival at Lacustre Largo, she had been confronted with the incarnation of her own stupid ignorance . . .

Once her acceptance of Miguel's proposal had been formalized, her life had seemed to resemble a ski-run with herself as the skier at the head of the slope. Once she was embarked on her course, however, Miguel allowed nothing and no one to stand in her way, and everything happened so quickly that she was not given time to have second thoughts even had she dared to have any. He had instituted a telephone call to her father in Perisoire, a suburb of Montreal, and Emma had stammered out her reasons for breaking with Victor and marrying Miguel Salvaje in a matter of minutes. Naturally, she had not given her father the whole truth, and she sensed his anxiety. But when she went on to explain that they were flying to Montreal on their way to Mexico, he had sounded much more enthusiastic.

After that, there was nothing to stand in their way. Emma attended medical examinations, submitted to inoculations, and generally prepared for the journey. But she was in a daze most of the time and Mrs. Cook found the whole affair most disturbing. She was no longer antagonistic towards Miguel, but she sensed he had some hold over her employer's daughter, and on one occasion told him outright that he had better take good care of her. Miguel had seemed amused by the incident, but Emma had found herself unable to discuss it with him. She had told herself that things would change, that once they were married they would achieve the closeness which seemed so lacking in their relationship, but it had not worked out like that.

The only person she could really talk to was Juan Castillo. Through her developing knowledge of Miguel's affairs, she had discovered that as well as being Miguel's manager, Juan was also his friend and assistant, and was capable of turning his hand to almost anything. He was the only person who seemed to understand the strain that was being put upon her at this time, and he did his best to make things easier for her.

But only Miguel could really do that, and she had seen little of him in those days before the wedding. They were married in a simple civil ceremony. It was a very quiet affair with only Juan and Loren Delmar and Paul Gregory present, the information not being given to the press until after it was all over. Emma wore the blue slack suit and a rather attractive blue hat with a broad brim, but it was not like a wedding, and she certainly didn't feel any different afterwards, particularly as Miguel had only bent to kiss her forehead before urging her outside.

There was a small reception at Miguel's hotel attended by one or two friends and some musicians from the orchestra, at which Miguel announced that he and Emma would be having a church wedding once they were back in Mexico, but that was the first she had heard of it. Then the cake was cut, good wishes were given, and soon only Paul, Loren and Juan remained of their guests.

Emma was terribly nervous, and dreaded the moment when they would be alone. For all he attracted her so devastatingly, she had never shared any kind of intimacy with a man before, and the idea of getting undressed before him, of him having the right to share her room and her bed, terrified her. She didn't know what she felt about him that day; he had seemed like a stranger to her, and she desperately yearned for a little time to be alone, to gather her thoughts and her composure.

But she need not have been alarmed, had she but known it. The evening of that momentous day in her life was no different from the evening she had spent at the hotel when she told Miguel she would marry him. Paul stayed until eleven, by which time Loren had gone to bed, but Juan showed no signs of leaving them. On the contrary, after Paul had gone he took some papers out of a briefcase and he and Miguel began discussing them almost as though Emma wasn't there.

Eventually Juan seemed to sense her unwilling presence, and standing up, suggested to Miguel that he showed her where she was to sleep. Emma had expected some reaction from this, some effort on Miguel's part to be alone with her, but although her heart fluttered alarmingly, and her knees became shaky beneath her, Miguel merely made a casually assenting gesture and Juan indicated that she should go with him.

She was not shown, as she had expected, into Miguel's room. Instead, she entered one of the other bedrooms where her case stood waiting for her to unpack it. It was a beautiful bedroom, warmly decorated in shades of pink and gold, with an enormous double bed, but to Emma it was cold and unwelcomingly.

She remembered now how she had lain awake for hours waiting for Miguel to appear, shivering in the nylon wraper she had daringly bought herself for her wedding night.

But he did not appear. And eventually she supposed she must have fallen asleep, for she was awakened by Juan with her breakfast on a tray.

If, in those early days, she had thought about Miguel's family at all, it was to assume that they knew what he was doing, and that none of them had attended the wedding did not seem so surprising in the circumstances. After all, they were returning to Mexico almost immediately, and several thousand miles was a tremendous distance to travel just for a couple of days.

But the pattern of their life together so far had been set. Just like Juan Castillo and Loren Delmar, she was treated as another member of his entourage, but without the consideration they received. On the contrary, it appeared that Miguel was avoiding her and only when some outsider was present did he seem to behave more naturally. She couldn't understand it, and, hurt and miserable, she withdrew into a shell she had erected around herself. Not even the magnificent trousseau which Miguel had insisted she bought before leaving London could compensate for the knowledge that in some way he had induced her to marry him without feeling anything for her whatsoever. He simply wasn't the same man who had taken her out on the dunes and made passionate love to her, and her mind ached with the constant torment of trying to find reasons for what he had done.

She didn't see Victor again, although Mrs. Cook had told her that he had called several times. But she was never available. Miguel saw to that, even though he might not be with her at the time.

They left for Montreal on Saturday morning, and that, for Emma, was another revelation. It appeared that Miguel's father owned his own aircraft, and it was this small, sleek jet which transported them across the Atlantic. The interior of the plane resembled nothing so much as a lounge and there was every luxury provided for their comfort. Emma couldn't help but feel excited at seeing her father again, but when she mentioned this in one of her rare moments alone with Miguel he merely smiled enigmatically and said that they would only have a couple of hours to spare.

Crushing her disappointment, Emma wondered what her father would make of her changed appearance. In the soft feminine clothes Loren Delmar had helped to choose for her she looked vastly different from the severely dressed young woman who had used to accompany Victor everywhere. Now she looked young and almost beautiful, but so far as her husband was concerned she might never have bothered.

Montreal was like any other big city, impersonal and traffic-jammed. A taxi transported Emma and Miguel to her brother's house in the suburbs, but by the time they reached their destination half their allotted time had been wasted. In consequence their conversation had to be brief, but at least Emma was assured of one thing: her father thought she was happy. And indeed with Miguel behaving in the charming way he was capable of doing she was happy. But as soon as they left he reverted to his usual detachment and she hadn't the courage to ask what was wrong.

They flew on to Mexico in the late afternoon, arriving at Mexico City's international airport late at night. But here one of Miguel's father's limousines was waiting for them and this took them into Mexico City itself where they spent the night at another luxury hotel.

They spent three days in Mexico City while Miguel saw specialists about his injured fingers and Juan conducted some business of his own. As far as Emma was aware, no one contacted Miguel's family while they stayed in Mexico City, and this surprised her somewhat. But she was too eager to get used to the rarefied atmosphere and take in the warmth and beauty of her surroundings to pay much attention to anything else.

She got to know Loren rather better, too. Although she doubted they could ever be close friends, nevertheless, being of a similar age and left to their own devices, they went about a lot together. Loren knew the city well, of course, and so long as they avoided personal topics they could spend many interesting hours together. Emma came to know Chapultepec Park and the Paseo de la Reforma almost as well as the Mexican girl, and they spent hours in the Museum of Anthropology studying the fascinating remains of the mingled cultures that had helped to shape Mexico's development. They saw the murals, too, at the National Palace which were painted by the Indian patriot, Diego Rivera. They depicted the story of the conquest of the Aztecs by Hernando Cortes and his Spanish *conquistadores*, and Emma, used to hearing the story from other sources deploring the human sacrifices made by these primitive Indian tribes, was almost shocked to be told that Cortes was the usurper, destroying a civilization far in advance of its time. The guide was Indian, of course, and she was quite glad to emerge into the sunlight again and realize that it had all happened more than four hundred years ago.

More humbling an experience was entering the imposing Cathedral, the oldest Christian building in the Americas, built over the ruins of the Aztecs' Great Temple.

They eventually left Mexico City on Wednesday afternoon, this time travelling by helicopter, bound for Puebla, which was the nearest big city to Lacustre Largo.

The nearer they drew to Miguel's home, the more morose he seemed to become, and Emma couldn't understand it. She wished he would just talk to her, share with her a little the fears and apprehensions she was experiencing in this strange and alien environment. She needed him more with every mile they travelled, while he seemed to need her less and less . . .

The country over which they were flying was rather terrifying, too. Mountains and gorges, inland lakes and fertile valleys, the whole possessing a wild and savage beauty that Emma had never seen before. Miguel sat up front with the pilot while she, Loren and Juan were closely pressed together behind. If Miguel spoke at all it was to the pilot or to Juan, who, while seeming to appreciate Emma's anxieties, could in no way alleviate them.

They landed on a private airfield at Puebla in the late afternoon. Emma, who had eaten practically nothing all day, was feeling hot and a little faint, but no one seemed to notice. The owner of the airfield turned out to be a man called Felipe Alvarez, a big fat individual who welcomed Miguel like a son and proceeded to ignore everyone else.

Juan seemed unconcerned. 'We will have a meal here,' he explained to Emma, as she smoothed the white skirt she was wearing over her slim hips and watched her husband disappearing into the airfield buildings with Felipe Alvarez.

'Will we?' Emma's tone was dry and she endeavoured to hide her frustration. 'Then what?'

'Then we fly on to Lacustre Largo,' announced Juan firmly.

The meal Alvarez's wife provided was not to Emma's taste. Until then she had managed quite well with the highly spiced food, choosing only those dishes she had known and recognized. But the *tortillas,* stuffed with meat and onion and tomato, and served with a thick spicy tomato and chilli sauce, were far too rich, and she had to swallow mouthfuls of the liquid they were given to drink to get anything down. It wasn't until afterwards when her head felt slightly swimmy that she realized that what she had been drinking must have been alcoholic.

She remembered little of the journey from Puebla to Lacustre Largo except waking up once with her head on Juan's shoulder to find Miguel remonstrating angrily with him in Spanish about something which she couldn't understand. But it was dark anyway, and there was nothing much to see.

They landed some distance from the house and now Emma was wide awake. She could vaguely make out the silhouette of Miguel's father's home and there were lights and the sound of voices almost before the helicopter was fully landed. Shimmering away to the left was a stretch of water painted palely now by the moon and she supposed that was Lake Largo, Lacustre Largo, from which the house got its unusual name.

With the propellers slowing, Miguel thrust back his door and climbed out, standing for a moment looking out towards the lake. Then he turned and began to help Loren disembark. Juan was last, and he took a deep breath of the sharp air, savouring it like wine.

'*Marvilloso,*' he declared, with a smile at Emma. 'There

is nowhere like it.'

Miguel regarded them for a moment, dark and brooding in black slacks and a black silk shirt he had worn for travelling. Overall he wore a dark green suede waistcoat that hung loosely from his shoulders, and Emma thought he had never looked more attractive or more alien.

'Come,' he said, taking Emma's arm, surprising her by this gesture. 'I will take you to meet my father.'

Emma went with him, as much out of curiosity as anything else. She noticed he had not mentioned his mother or the other members of his family and decided that in Mexican households the man of the family was obviously considered of supreme importance. She wasn't altogether sure she agreed with this premise.

They crossed a sweep of grass before the house which Emma could now see stood on a rise of ground, stone built, with the sloping roof of a hacienda. It was a split-level dwelling, she saw, thickly surrounded by tropical foliage which in daylight would look quite startlingly beautiful.

But for the moment her surroundings were of secondary importance to what was before her. Before they could reach the house, however, several servants appeared, chattering excitedly in their own language, which Miguel answered with good-natured fluidity, obviously glad to see him back again. The Indian girls were dark-eyed and dark-skinned, peeping at Emma curiously, clearly speculating as to her identity. Emma wondered if Miguel's father had told them that his son had married an English girl.

Juan and Loren were following them and they mounted the shallow stone steps, crossed the terrace, and entered through an arched doorway into the hall. It was tiled in a blue and gold mosaic, and the walls were exquisitely painted in murals illustrating Indian art in its most moving form. It was an intricate design of costume and craft and humanity. Although the lighting was electric, the lamps through which it filtered were again of Indian design, and the vase supporting some exotic orchids appeared to be of Aztec origin.

Emma stared about her in wonder as Miguel released her to speak to one of the manservants hovering about him. It was all so spacious, so beautiful, so vastly different from even her wildest imaginings. Imagine being born here.

She returned her attention to her husband as Juan and Loren came into the hall, and hearing the word *padre* in Miguel's conversation realized that he must be asking where his father was. Surely no one could not have heard the helicopter overhead.

And then, as though Carlos Salvaje had just heard the sound of his son's voice, or perhaps the sudden upheaval of his house had attracted his attention, he came striding through a doorway to their right, and walking up to Miguel, embraced him warmly and passionately. This was undoubtedly Miguel's father, Emma realized. He was tall, like his son, and the facial resemblance between them was pronounced, but whereas Miguel's hair was dark, his father's was turning grey, and the older man's body was looser, less muscular.

'Miguel! *Mi hijo, mi hijo,*' he cried, his voice husky with emotion, and Emma felt a lump in her throat watching them. Then Carlos drew back to look searchingly at his son. Lifting Miguel's injured hand, he shook his head. '*Que tragedia!*' he muttered fiercely, and then went on to talk swiftly in Spanish so that Emma lost all track of what they were saying.

But gradually Miguel drew away from his father and Carlos paid attention to the other members of the group standing in the hall. He spoke warmly to Loren and to Juan, but his gaze lingered longest on Emma and there was no doubt about his surprise at seeing her there.

Emma's stomach plunged, and she had the first inkling

that everything was not as it should be. Carlos turned to his son and in rapid Spanish asked who she was.

Then Miguel came across to her, putting an arm protectively across her shoulders. 'We will speak English, *padre*,' he said quietly. 'My wife speaks very little Spanish.'

'*Your wife!*' There was bitter disbelief in Carlos's angry protest. 'Miguel, you cannot be serious!'

'But I am,' replied Miguel calmly, and Emma sensed the pleasure he was gaining from telling his father this. 'Are you not going to congratulate me?'

Emma slid out of bed now. She could not bear to remain there any longer. She walked to the long windows and releasing the catch stepped out on to the terrace. She cared little that the air was cool and that all she was wearing was the chiffon nightgown she had bought on the Avenida Insurgentes in Mexico City. The coldness she felt came from within, not without, and no one was likely to see her here at this hour of the night. Everyone was asleep.

She thought back over the last few hours with chilled foreboding. Juan had told her that Miguel had a mother – brothers – sisters – but where were they? The only other person who appeared to share this house with Carlos Salvaje was his niece, Miguel's cousin, Carmen Silveiro.

Emma shivered. She had not liked Carmen Silveiro, and it was certain that Carmen did not like her. Like her uncle, she had been ignorant of Miguel's marriage to the English girl, and her greeting to him had been warmly possessive. Carmen was very beautiful and very Spanish, small and dark and exotic, her hair a cap of ebony silk. She made Emma feel tall and ungainly, although that was only her opinion. She had thrown herself into her cousin's arms only a few minutes after Miguel had exploded the shock of his marriage on his father when they were all still standing there looking at one another, and the kiss she had given him had been more than just cousinly.

But when Carlos had passionately informed her of the facts the change in her had been quite remarkable. Her olive cheeks had paled and the glance she had cast in Emma's direction had been purely malevolent.

The scents from the flowers below the terrace invaded Emma's senses, and she stretched her arms disconsolately, longing for the peace of mind she seemed to have forfeited for ever. The cry of the mountain lion came again, and she stiffened. Perhaps if she remained here it would come for her and destroy her, and take away this misery that was engulfing her once and for all. Then she would not have to see Carlos Salvaje again, not have to bear witness to his extreme displeasure with his son for marrying without his permission, not have to share this house with people who she knew desposed her — not least of these being her own husband ...

She leant wearily against the terrace wall, her hands spread dejectedly along the stonework, the rounded contours of her body outlined through the filmy chiffon, her hair, silvered by the moon, cloaking her slender shoulders with heavy silk.

'*Dios!* Emma, have you taken leave of your senses?'

Emma almost jumped out of her skin at the unexpected sound of Miguel's voice, low and angry, behind her. She turned slowly, one hand pressed to her throat, and looked at him as though she couldn't really believe he was there, as though he were some figment of her imagination conjured up out of the depths of her despair.

'Miguel,' she murmured faintly.

'What are you doing out here?' he demanded, stepping towards her, and now she could see he was still fully dressed in the black clothes he had worn to travel in.

'I — I couldn't sleep,' she replied unsteadily, becoming conscious of the scarcity of her own covering. A chiffon nightgown was hardly the thing to confront an irate husband, she thought hysterically. Or perhaps it was. Perhaps that was how woman's weakness overcame man's strength.

The roar of the mountain lion sounded closer now, and Emma glanced round almost fearfully, as though she half expected to find the animal behind her.

'You had better go inside,' said Miguel, indicating the opened glass doors of her bedroom. 'The puma has been known to seek the more civilized districts of this area in search of its kill.'

Emma looked at him tremulously. 'Do you think I care?'

'What do you mean?'

'I wish it would come here – I wish it would come – *for me!*' Her voice broke and she half turned away from him, unwilling for him to see her distress.

'You don't know what you're saying,' he muttered, his accent thickening. 'Emma – please to go back to bed.'

She moved her head slowly from side to side, and he swore softly before saying: 'I insist you do as I ask.'

Emma put up a hand and massaged the nape of her neck tiredly, unaware how the careless action drew attention to the pointed swell of her breasts. But Miguel was aware of it, and in a tormented voice, he said: '*Madre de Dios*, Emma, do as I say!'

'Why?' She looked at him out of the corners of her eyes. 'Why should I do anything you ask? Do you realize this is the first time we've been really alone together since that night in your hotel suite?' She shivered involuntarily. 'Just go away and leave me alone!'

Miguel clenched his fists. 'You're cold. Do you want to get pneumonia?'

'I don't particularly care,' she answered huskily, bending her head.

Miguel moved then, taking the space between them in a couple of strides, sliding his arms around her from behind, dragging her roughly back against him. Emma resisted only for a moment, and then the warmth and urgency of his body invaded hers, and she let herself yield against him.

'*Dios, esta demente!*' he groaned thickly, his mouth moving against the soft curve of her shoulder, bared by his fingers as they pushed the offending chiffon aside. Emma knew those words, they meant that what he was doing was insane, but he didn't stop. Instead, he twisted her round in his arms and then his mouth was on hers, all fire and passion and hungry need. Her lips parted willingly, and weakness made her cling to him so that he slid his arms beneath her and swung her up against him, carrying her across the terrace and into the quiet intimacy of her bedroom. He laid her on the bed, and as though the action had brought him to his senses he tried to straighten up again. But Emma's arms were about his neck, and when he would have drawn away she pulled him down to her, seeking his mouth with hers.

Miguel lost his head then, bearing her back against the silken bed-coverings, possessing her mouth with a passion that weakened and yet terrified her. It was one thing to want the man one loved, and she knew she loved him now, to make love to her, and quite another to realize that he was virtually a stranger to her who had married her for some nefarious purpose of his own. She knew so little about him, and when he began to unbutton his shirt and she felt the hardness of his flesh against hers, she panicked. Taking advantage of his sensually induced weakness, she pulled herself away from him and slid off the bed at the other side, stumbling across the room to stand panting against the far wall. Contrarily, once she had left him, she longed to be back in his arms again, but when she looked towards the bed and saw Miguel still lying there, she could not move.

There was a moment's stillness, and then with a shrug

Miguel fastened his clothes and slid off the bed himself, looking across at her intently. She could not make out his expression, his face was in shadow, but she sensed his contempt.

'Perhaps now you will appreciate the dangers of wandering about the terrace without adequate covering!' he said, with bitter mockery.

'Miguel, I—'

'Don't say anything else!' he commanded, and turning, walked out through the long glass doors, sliding them together with a definite click.

CHAPTER NINE

THE following morning, Emma had the opportunity of seeing quite a lot more of her husband's domain.

She must have slept for some time after Miguel had left, for she was awakened by one of the smiling Indian girls soon after eight o'clock with a tray of coffee and hot rolls and butter. She struggled up in bed to take the tray, blinking in the sunlight that streamed through the windows, and although she felt sure she would be unable to eat a thing, the rolls smelt so delicious she couldn't resist trying them.

Afterwards, she thrust the tray aside and rushed to the long windows for her first glimpse of the grounds in daylight. But before lingering there she pulled a cord to the right of the windows which the maid had shown her the night before and which caused a swathe of ruched nylon curtain to slide across the windows providing her with privacy from outside.

The brilliance of the garden was not subdued in the bright sunlight, and beyond the terrace where several shades of bougainvillea twined, there were oleanders and creamy magnolias, and vivid splashes of hibiscus. There were lots of other flowering shrubs which Emma had never seen before, the whole giving an impression of wild cultivation and lush tropicality.

Stretches of lawn, interspersed with mosaic paths and small flowering trees, led down to the wide waters of the lake, which shaded from turquoise to deepest blue. Beyond the lake, the high reaches of the Sierra Madre cast their own shadows, a fitting backcloth for so much colour and fertility.

Leaving the window with reluctance, Emma sought the

coolness of her bathroom, marvelling again as she had the night before, at its tiled luxury. As well as the usual accoutrements there was a round step-in bath, big enough for half a dozen adults, and a shower. The tiles were in various shades of blue and green, and there were mirrors everywhere, giving her back her reflection in a thousand different ways.

Later, she dressed in yellow cotton pants and a sleeveless ribbed yellow jumper, and went in search of the other members of the household. It took a great deal of courage to leave the sanctuary of her room, but it had to be done and there was no point pretending otherwise. She simply refused to let Miguel see how much he could hurt her.

Soft rubber tiles cushioned her feet as she followed the passage back towards the lounge they had entered the night before. She had to descend several steps to reach that level, the bedrooms being above the servants' quarters on the higher level.

But the lounge was deserted and she looked about her distractedly, not quite knowing what to do. Somehow this room was not the sort of place one could relax in alone with its intricately carved ceiling and frescoed walls. The highly polished wooden floor was strewn with animal skins, while all the furniture was of palest hide. The cabinet in one corner which housed a collection of silver and porcelain must have been worth a small fortune, while there was a picture above the wide, tapestry-screened fireplace which she suspected was priceless. But where else could she go? She didn't know the layout of the house well enough to explore.

And then, as though in answer to a silent prayer, she heard the sound of footsteps crossing the hall and swung round in relief. But that relief was tempered when she encountered Carlos Salvaje's brooding stare.

He regarded her for a long moment, taking in the de-

135

licious picture she made, all in yellow, her tawny hair loose and catching the vibrant rays of the sun. Then he said politely: '*Buenos dias, señorita – señora!*'

'Good – good morning, *señor.*' Emma did not trust herself to speak his language in case he assumed she was conversant with it.

'You slept well?'

Emma hesitated. 'Quite well, thank you.' She glanced round, gesticulating awkwardly towards the garden. 'It's a beautiful morning.'

'We have many such mornings,' commented Carlos curtly.

'Yes. Yes, I suppose you have.' Emma endeavoured to remain cool. 'I'm afraid I'm used to a less reliable climate.'

Carlos raised his dark eyebrows at this, and her gaze flickered away from his face, taking in the fact that he was dressed for riding in pale grey breeches and black, shiny boots, a cream shirt open at his strong throat. Miguel would look like this in perhaps thirty years' time, she thought perceptively, and her heart lurched when she considered what that thirty years might mean to her.

'You have had *desayuno*?' he asked, tapping the short whip he held in his hand against his boot.

'Breakfast?' Emma nodded vigorously. 'Yes. A maid brought it to my room.'

'That is good.' Carlos considered her thoughtfully. 'Do you ride, *señora*?'

Emma caught her breath. 'Please – call me Emma,' she said. 'And yes, I have ridden. Although not for several years, I'm afraid.'

'It is not something one forgets.' Carlos inclined his head. 'Very well then – Emma. Would you care to accompany me this morning? I want to ride over to the village to see my – how do you say it – *mandatario*? Manager?'

'I'm afraid I don't have any riding clothes.' Emma made a helpless movement of her shoulders. 'Much as I should like to come with you . . .'

Carlos frowned, his dark eyes, so like Miguel's, assessing her appearance. 'Surely what you are wearing now, together with some stronger shoes—' He pointed his whip towards her thonged sandals with distaste. 'You have some boots, perhaps?'

Emma glanced down at her feet. 'Yes, I have some boots.'

'Good.' He tapped his boot again with his whip. 'Come outside when you are ready.' And he turned and strode away across the hall again.

Emma gazed after him with some misgiving. If only Miguel were here to advise her – or Juan. Someone else to consult before going with this tall, arrogant stranger.

But there was no one else about, and she dared not keep him waiting. Besides, if she was really honest with herself, she knew she wanted to go. After all, this was Miguel's father, and there was something exciting about the prospect of spending a morning exploring the magnificent country-side beyond the formal grounds of the house.

She put on cream suede boots, allowing her trouser legs to fall over them, and then rummaged in her bag for the dark glasses she had bought in Mexico City. Huge frames accen-tuated the pure lines of her oval face, and the girl reflected in her dressing-table mirror was almost as much a stranger to her as Carlos Salvaje.

Collecting a chunky white cardigan, she made her way back to the hall and passed through the arched doorway on to the terrace, which ran all round the house, with particular areas bracketed by trellis-work intertwined with the ubiqui-tous bougainvillea.

She saw her host some distance away round the side of the building talking to one of the Indian servants, and she tried not to walk too eagerly towards him. However, he saw her coming and dismissed the man with casual ease. Then, when Emma had joined him, he said: 'Come: the stables are through these trees. I have had José saddle Candida for you. She is a quiet mare, not given to violent fits of passion.' His expression had softened slightly, but Emma sensed it was because he loved his horses and not for any other reason.

His own horse Nubarro was a vastly different proposition. Tall and dark like its master, Nubarro possessed a fiery, excitable nature, evident in its flashing eyes and stamping impatience, and Emma, unused to such spirited temper, avoided its restless hooves as she was helped on to Candida's back.

It was very hot, and she was draping her unwanted cardigan across the front of her saddle when Carlos leant across and handed her a worn cream sombrero. 'Put it on,' he directed. 'It will protect the back of your neck.'

Emma shrugged, but she slipped the hat on to her head, noticing as she did so that Carlos apparently needed nothing. But then he was used to the sun.

They cantered out of the stable area and down the grassy slope towards the lake. Emma took her first real gulp of pure mountain air and sighed in delight. In the distance, across the lake, she could see a small boat with two occupants, and Carlos allowed her mare to come alongside him and commented that the water was good for fishing.

They followed the line of the lake for some distance before branching off to trek a short way beside a gurgling stream. It cascaded down the mountainside, splashing over rocks and fernlike growths, as clear as tap water. The air was filled with the sounds of the birds and other animals, and bees hummed busily from one exotic bloom to another. Every now and then Carlos made some comment concerning their surroundings, but mostly he left Emma to simply enjoy the beauty of the day.

It was getting much hotter, and she was glad of the sombrero, although she looked rather concernedly at Carlos's bare head.

'You don't wear a hat,' she said, and he shook his head.

'Sometimes,' he conceded. Then, as though by her question she had broken the silence between them, he went on: 'Tell me: what has Miguel told you about me?'

Emma's fingers tightened on Candida's reins. 'Not a lot,' she admitted awkwardly.

Carlos studied her bent head. 'You were not curious about his family?'

'Of course I was curious.' Emma sighed and looked at him. 'Where is his mother – your wife?'

Carlos's mouth tightened. 'I have no wife,' he replied harshly.

Emma absorbed this with difficulty. 'You have no wife?' She shook her head. 'You mean – you are divorced?'

'My wife is dead.'

Emma stared at him in surprise. 'But – but Juan said—'

Carlos's eyes hardened. 'Yes? What did Juan say?'

She flushed. 'Oh, nothing.'

'But yes, I insist.' He cantered close to her. 'What did Juan tell you?'

Emma drew a trembling breath. 'It's not important.' But it was! Juan had said Miguel's mother was alive; that he had brothers and sisters! He *had* said that.

Carlos looked as though he was about to argue with her further, but then he looked away, and said: 'Miguel was born here, at Lacustre Largo, in the bed in which I myself was born.'

Emma was interested in spite of herself. 'He's very lucky.'

'Yes.' Carlos said the word slowly. Then: 'Perhaps he does not think so.' His lips twisted. 'I do not always understand him.'

That makes two of us, thought Emma dryly, but she didn't say it. Instead, she said: 'This village we are going to – what is it called?'

'Largo,' said Carlos briefly, guiding Nubarro between a clump of jacarandas, their blossoms scenting the air, fluttering to make a pale carpet at their feet. 'Miguel tells me you are to have a wedding in the church here in Puebla.'

'He told you that?' Emma played for time.

'Yes. Last night, before he went to bed. I regret keeping him so late. We talked until the early hours of this morning.'

That explained why Miguel was still dressed when he found her on the terrace, thought Emma, looking up at the network of branches above their heads. She wondered what they had talked about for so long. What had Miguel told his father about them, about their meeting for the first time, the reasons for their marriage? Had Miguel explained the circumstances surrounding his injuries, for example? Had he any idea of the difficulties she was likely to encounter when she didn't even know what he was thinking?

In the distance she could see some houses now, small, single-storied dwellings, curls of smoke rising from their chimneys in spite of the heat of the day. Nodding towards them, she asked: 'Is this Largo?'

Carlos nodded. 'Yes, this is the village. No doubt you will find it all rather primitive after England. Unfortunately, people here either cannot, or will not, improve their lot.'

It was primitive. Emma tried not to let Carlos see how appalled she was by the houses which were little more than thatched-roofed huts jostling together beneath the trees beside the mud-baked track. Open doorways gave glimpses of bare interiors where a charcoal stove was the only means of cooking, while half-naked children played in the dirt with a complete disregard for sanitation. There were few men to be seen and Emma guessed this was because they were all away working in the fields or wherever else they might be employed, but the women, who all seemed to wear the same type of peasant blouse and full skirt, bobbed before Carlos and herself as if they were visiting royalty.

'You see,' said Carlos, pointing with his whip towards one of the huts. 'They live like animals, or perhaps that is an unfair analogy. Animals, generally speaking, take more care of their young.'

Emma felt repelled by the cold indifference in his voice, and yet at the same time she recognized what he was saying was the truth. 'But how do they sleep?' she exclaimed.

Carlos indicated the straw mats which littered the floor of the huts. 'They sleep on those,' he said. 'They are called *petates*. It is all they have ever known.'

Emma was amazed. She would never have believed that human beings, so close to a modern civilization, could live so primitively, changing little over the centuries.

Clearing her throat, she said: 'Where does this man live who we are going to see?'

'It is not far now,' he replied. 'Just beyond the village.'

Emma was not sorry to leave the village behind, and now she could see ahead of them some distance up the track, the white-daubed walls of an adobe house. Two-storied, with curtains at the windows, it contrasted violently with the primitive dwellings in the village, and Emma looked at Carlos in surprise.

'Alfaro Diaz is a good worker,' he commented. 'He has been in my employ for many years now.'

'And he – looks after the estate?'

'Part of it, yes. But I employ many people, Emma. One manager would not be enough.'

She nodded slowly, and as they neared the house some children appeared and came running down the track to greet them. There were three, the eldest perhaps ten, the youngest no more than five or six. Carlos dismounted, a good-natured smile softening his stern features.

'Ah, *chiquillos*!' he exclaimed, leading his horse as he approached them. Then he dropped the reins and gathered the youngest up into his arms, laughing and talking to him in rapid Spanish.

Hesitantly, Emma dismounted too and followed his example, aware of the speculative stares of the other children. The youngest was a boy, but the others were girls, dark-haired and dark-eyed, and yet not Indian in appearance. Obviously their parents were of Spanish extraction.

Carlos glanced round at her. 'Come!' he said imperatively, putting the boy on his feet again. 'Meet my little ones. See, this is Rosita – Cecilia, and this – Clemente.'

Emma smiled at the children. '*Buenos dias!*' she said.

'*Buenos dias, señorita,*' they chorused politely, clearly unaware of the significance of the broad gold band on her third finger.

Carlos reverted to Spanish and asked the children where their parents were. Emma, gradually gathering the meanings of certain words and phrases, was able to understand this.

A small garden hedged about with a shrubbery surrounded the Diaz house, and Emma preceded Carlos up the garden path to the door which stood wide to the air. Stretching ahead of them was a cool, tiled passage, and from this passage all the ground floor rooms of the house opened. A wooden staircase at the end of the hall led to the upper storey and Emma saw how meticulously clean everything was, the polished wood gleaming, the tiles bright and shining.

The children had gone ahead of them and as Emma and Carlos reached the door a man appeared in the hall. 'Don Carlos!' he exclaimed, in surprise, his gaze flickering towards Emma. '*Que sorpresa!*'

'*Buenos dias*, Alfaro!' said Carlos, urging Emma before him into the house. '*Esta bien?*'

'*Si, si—*' Alfaro was clearly not prepared for this intrusion, and Emma was beginning to wish she had not agreed to come.

Then beyond the man, a woman appeared. She was tall and slender, with serene, madonna-like features. When she saw Carlos, she smiled, and in lilting Spanish bade them come in.

They entered the kitchen of the house, a large, well-lit room, which obviously served as dining-room too. A long scrubbed table was flanked by wooden forms and chairs, and the huge fireplace was hung about with gleaming pots and pans. The woman, who Emma guessed was Señora Diaz, chased several children out of another door which apparently led to the back of the house and then bade her guests sit down. She had looked at Emma several times, quick darting glances with nothing of hostility in them, and yet Emma sensed her unease. But why this woman should feel uneasy about her she could not imagine.

Carlos drew Emma forward, his hands cool on her bare arms. Speaking in English, he said: 'Maria – Alfaro; I'd like to introduce you to Emma – Emma Salvaje, Miguel's *wife!*'

The stupefaction in their faces was ludicrous and Emma, uncertain as to how to respond to that introduction, stood nervously, waiting for someone else to make the first move. The steady ticking of a clock on the shelf above the wide fireplace seemed magnified in the sudden, still air, and the sounds of the children playing in the garden seemed distant and unreal. A cat which had been curled up on the hearth arched its back and stood upright before slinking away outside as though disturbed by the uncanny silence which had fallen. It was as though they were players on a stage who had all forgotten their lines.

Maria Diaz was the first to move. Realizing that something was expected of her, she held out her hand and Emma took it. 'I am most pleased to meet you,' she said, in stilted English.

Emma managed a smile, although the tensions in the room were almost tangible. Then Alfaro Diaz followed his wife's lead and taking her hand repeated what Maria had said, adding that Miguel was a lucky man.

But it was all so stiff and uncomfortable, and Emma longed for Carlos to say that they could go. What was there about that announcement which could cause such unexpected strain between them? Had these people a daughter whom they had expected Miguel to marry? Did that account for the strange little smile playing about Carlos Salvaje's lips?

There were a few more moments of awkward silence, and then Carlos took command. It was as though he had enjoyed their shocked incredulity long enough. Like a cat who becomes bored with the antics of its prey. 'Are you not going to offer us some of your most excellent coffee, Maria?' he asked, his eyes chiding her. 'Believe me, it was just as much a – surprise to me as it was to you.'

Emma sank down into a chair, and as she did so she intercepted a look Alfaro Diaz cast in Carlos's direction. His eyes conveyed a combination of dislike and frustration and then he flung himself towards the door.

'Excuse me, *señora*,' he said, speaking to Emma, 'but I have work to do.' And without speaking to Carlos he went out, the door banging behind him.

Emma quivered. This was all too much for her to understand, and on impulse she got up and went towards the back door, stepping out into the sunlight with a sense of relief. Carlos and Maria were talking together, she could hear them, but their conversation was too swift, too staccato, for her to understand. But she sensed that Maria was remonstrating with him in some way.

There were five children in the garden. Two older boys had joined the younger children, and they were kicking a football about energetically, laughing together. They stopped when they saw Emma and stared at her curiously. Wishing she knew more of the language, Emma pointed to the ball, gesticulating that they should allow her to join their game.

There was a few moments' hesitation, and then one of the older boys grinned and picking up the ball tossed it to her. Emma had to duck to avoid it hitting her, but taking her cue from them she tossed it back again and soon there was quite a lively interchange going on. She had shed her sombrero in the house, but now she began to wish she had it on as the sun beat down unmercifully.

At last she had to seek the shade of the doorway, and as she backed into the kitchen, waving at the children, Carlos came behind her and said: 'Come and have some coffee. I have been telling Maria of the romantic way in which you met my son.'

Emma turned reluctantly, but there was a look of such entreaty on Maria Diaz' face that she smiled and accepted a chair, and took a mug of the deliciously smelling beverage from her hand.

Choosing her words carefully, Emma parried Maria's gentle probing, realizing that this woman must be very fond of Miguel. It was evident in the way she spoke of him, in the intense interest she showed in everything Emma said. Emma wondered if she disapproved of him marrying an English girl as much as Carlos did.

And yet did he? she asked herself. She didn't really understand Carlos any more than she understood his son. This morning he had seemed so human somehow, so approachable, and only since they reached the Diaz house had there been any feeling of antagonism. And she couldn't altogether blame him for that.

Studying Maria surreptitiously in a moment when she was answering something Carlos had said to her, Emma wondered how old she was. There was an agelessness about her features that could have put her age anywhere between thirty-five and fifty-five, but Emma guessed it was somewhere in between. She must have been a beautiful girl, she thought, for she was still a beautiful woman, and while Alfaro Diaz might be of mixed blood, Maria surely could not. She had the pure, classic skin of a Spaniard, and even dressed in homespun cotton she had a definite air of breeding. It was puzzling, and Emma had not the courage or the impertinence to question her.

At last Carlos said they could leave and Emma rose eagerly. During the past couple of hours she had succeeded in putting all thoughts of her own marriage to the back of her mind, but now they came flooding forward and she found herself impatient to get back to Lacustre Largo.

Maria came out to wave them good-bye, her children gathered about her skirts. They shouted after them gaily, and Emma was glad she had had the opportunity of spending some time with them. Children were so uncomplicated somehow.

The ride back to the house was accomplished almost in silence. Carlos seemed absorbed with his own thoughts, and like Miguel could cut himself off from those around him with the mental dropping of a shutter. Emma didn't particularly care. She had her own thoughts to occupy her, not least being the thought of confronting her husband after her stupidly adolescent behaviour of the night before.

Lacustre Largo dreamed in the heat of the midday sun. There was a deceptively tranquil air about it. As they neared the house, Carlos suggested that Emma should dismount and he would see their horses into the stables, and she was glad to do so. The ride back had not been so comfortable for her, and her muscles were protesting at so much activity.

She ran up the steps into the hall almost eagerly, but then halted abruptly when her husband came through one of the arched doorways that led off the hall and grasping her arm in a cruel grip, demanded: 'Where the devil do you think you've been?'

Emma struggled to free herself, but it was useless. 'If you must know, I've been riding – with your father!' she declared triumphantly.

'Riding? With my father?' Miguel glared at her furiously. 'Where did you ride?'

'I don't think that's any business of yours—'

'Damn you! Where did he take you?' Miguel's hold tightened and she could feel the blood draining out of her wrist.

'Let go of me, and I'll tell you!' she cried, trying to prise his fingers from her arm.

'*Tell me now!*' He was incensed, and she felt a trembling sense of fear invading her.

'We – we rode to the village—'

'What village?'

'L – Largo. We went to see a man who works—'

'Diaz!' muttered Miguel violently. 'Alfaro Diaz!'

'Yes, that's right,' said a mocking voice behind them, and glancing round Emma saw Carlos just entering the hall. 'Your wife enjoyed the outing, I am sure.'

Miguel was staring at his father now and there was concentrated hatred in his gaze. 'Why, you—' He bit off an epithet, and Carlos raised his dark eyebrows sardonically.

'Miguel!' he reproved. 'Remember, we are not alone. Is that any way for a son to speak to his father?'

Miguel let go of Emma's wrist so suddenly that she almost lost her balance, and stood rubbing it painfully, watching the two men as they faced one another.

'You never give up, do you, *padre*!' Miguel almost spat

the words.

'I don't know what you mean, Miguel,' returned Carlos, in pained tones. 'I can't think what I have done that should cause you so much annoyance. Surely after meeting your father, it was only right that Emma should meet your mother, was it not?'

CHAPTER TEN

THERE were five people for the light *colacion* which was served about two o'clock – Loren and Juan, Carmen and Carlos, and Emma. They ate in a small dining salon adjoining the lounge. Here the walls were plain and unadorned except for one or two exceptionally fine charcoal drawings which Juan explained had been done by a local artist. There was a main course of salad and minced pork, into which mashed avocado had been added, and fresh fruit and cheese to follow. Emma was unused to the variety of fresh fruits available such as apricots and pomegranates, and watched with distaste as Loren peeled the skin off the black flesh of a *zapote*.

They ate with the plaintive sounds of one of Chopin's sonatas drifting in through the open doorway, and every now and then a discordant cacophony of sound erupted as the pianist touched a wrong note and lost his temper.

Emma wondered if everyone else was as conscious of that music as she was. She ached with the desire to leave the table, to seek out the music room where Miguel was attempting to assuage his anguish, and show him in some way that what Carlos had done didn't matter in the least to her.

But how could she? He would never invite her sympathy and without an invitation she had not the right to thrust herself upon him. Besides, judging by the contempt he had shown her when she had arrived back at the house a couple of hours ago, she was the last person he would want to see.

She still felt a feeling of nausea when she recalled that scene in the hall. No wonder Carlos had seemed to behave so charmingly, no wonder Maria had been so shocked! He had smiled at their disbelief and taken sustenance from it.

Emma felt cold. It had been such a cruel thing to do. Not just to her, and to Miguel, but to Maria. Even now, she had no real knowledge of the truth as it actually was. She could only assume that at some time Carlos had had an affair with Maria and when their son was born he had adopted him.

But Carlos had also said that Miguel had been born in the bed where he himself had been born, and although his wife was dead now, where had she been at that time? Had she known of his affair with Maria? It seemed unnatural – uncivilized. She frowned and concentrated on the peach she was paring. That word kept cropping up, and yet these were civilized people.

There was a loud crash of bass notes and she started, her eyes going automatically towards the open door. Miguel ought not to be trying to play at all. His fingers were not healed yet. He could be doing irreparable damage. Didn't he care? Didn't anyone care?

She looked round the room despairingly and caught Carlos's eyes upon her. 'Something is wrong, Emma?' he queried silkily.

She clenched her fists. 'Someone should stop him,' she said. 'He shouldn't be touching the piano yet.'

Carlos lay back in his chair. 'And who do you suggest should tell him this? Me?' He pointed to himself. 'Or you?'

Emma glanced round. 'What about – Juan?'

Carlos raised his eyebrows. 'I think Juan knows better than that.'

Emma looked entreatingly at Miguel's manager, but he sighed and shook his head. Carmen Silveiro laughed, and it was not a pleasant sound.

'They are all scared of him, *señora*,' she said mockingly. 'When Miguel is angry it is best to stay out of his way.' Her

150

eyes were taunting. 'You do not know him very well or you would not suggest interfering. Miguel is angry – and unhappy. He has offended his father, and he regrets—'

'That will do, Carmen!' Carlos's voice was clipped and instantly silenced his niece. 'Now,' he went on, more gently, 'it is a glorious day. Let us enjoy it while we can. We will take our coffee out on to the terrace and perhaps drowse for a while, in the sun . . .'

But Emma could stand no more of it. Excusing herself from them, she made her way back to her room, going inside and closing the door almost as if by doing so she was shutting out the rest of the world.

But after a time, when she was sure the others would be firmly ensconced on the terrace, she left it again, and went in search of the music room.

Miguel was still playing and the sound seemed to come from further along the corridor, beyond her room and beyond Miguel's bedroom which she knew was the next bedroom along.

Smoothing her hair with her hands, she walked soundlessly down the passage until she stood before double doors from behind which the music was definitely emanating. She wondered whether to knock first or just walk in, but caution overcame all else and she rapped lightly on the panels. The melancholy strains of Brahms at his most appealing went on without cause and she realized he could not have heard her. Uncertainty gripped her. Her determination was ebbing with every minute that passed, and she dreaded the confrontation which might follow her intrusion.

Then a discordant note shattered the fragile melody and there was a muffled curse before silence descended on the room and the passage where Emma was standing.

Taking a deep breath, she turned the handle of the door and pushing it open squeezed into the room. Pressing against the wall, as if to disguise herself as part of the exquisite murals that depicted scenes of Mexico's fight for independence, she looked round in amazement. All the rooms in this house had astounded her by their individuality, and this was not least of them. A magnificent grand piano, at which Miguel was slumped, wholly unaware of her presence, was reflected in the polished wood of the floor, but as the ceiling was made up of dozens of squares of glass that in their turn reflected the floor, and also provided the wonderful acoustics, the instrument and its exponent were reflected over and over and over again. The jade green curtains at the long windows were drawn, however, and all the lighting in the room was artificial. Miguel had shut out everything and everybody.

The door clicked noisily as it closed and Emma froze. But he had heard it, and lifting his head he turned to stare at her almost uncomprehendingly. Then, as his brain cleared, he rose to his feet, tipping over the piano stool heavily on to the floor.

'What are you doing here?' he demanded. 'I thought I made it plain that I did not want to be disturbed.'

Emma straightened and moved away from the door. 'Why have you drawn the curtains?' she asked, playing for time. 'It's such a beautiful day outside.'

Miguel made an impatient gesture. 'I asked why you came! Did – my father – send you?'

Emma glanced at him, pretending an interest in the pile of manuscript on the piano. 'No. Why should he?'

Miguel sounded sceptical. 'Why not? I should have thought it was perfectly logical. He knows better than to come himself.'

Emma sighed. 'I came because I was concerned about you. You must know you could be doing your fingers irreparable damage by attempting to play the piano—'

'What business is that of yours?' He was cold.

'It's the business of anyone who appreciates your playing

– only it's obvious that no one else here—'

'I think you should leave now.'

'No!' Emma moved towards him. 'Miguel, be sensible! Don't behave like a spoilt child—'

'A spoilt child!' He glared at her bitterly. 'Is that what you think I am?'

'No! That is – well – oh, Miguel, why are you doing this? Can't you see how foolish it is? You're only hurting yourself—'

'*Bien*, that's something, isn't it? At least I don't interfere in other people's lives.'

'Meaning your father does.'

'You've noticed!' He was sarcastic.

'Oh, Miguel, if you mean what happened this morning—'

'What happened this morning was merely a continuation of what has been happening all my life!'

'It wasn't important—'

'It was. To me!'

'Miguel, if you think meeting your mother like that has shocked me—'

'Hasn't it?'

'No.' Emma flushed.

'I'm afraid I don't believe you. But it doesn't matter. What's done is done, and I can't make a better of it.'

'Your father loves you—'

'Oh, yes, yes.' Miguel's lips twisted. 'He does, doesn't he? Like the spider loves the fly – to destruction!'

'That's not true. Your father's not like that!'

'Isn't he?' He was bitter. 'Oh, I can see he's got a champion in you! How delighted he would be if he could hear you defending him – to me!'

'I'm not defending him,' she snapped hotly, hurt by his assumption that she was trying to take sides. 'I'm simply trying to make you see that by – behaving like this you're only making things more difficult for – for everyone!'

'What would you have me do?' he demanded coldly. 'Say — *gracias, padre,* for taking my wife to meet my mother without my prior knowledge or consent? *Gracias,* for showing her that my mother was never my father's wife!'

Emma sighed frustratedly. 'You should have told me yourself.'

Miguel clenched his uninjured fist and turned away. 'Oh, yes,' he muttered. 'Oh, yes. And have you any idea how?'

'But I was bound to find out—'

'Here? Yes! Yes, of course. You were meant to find out. I would have taken you to meet her. I wanted to be there when she met you for the first time. Strange as it may seem, Emma, I love my mother. I love my brothers and sisters. I just wish to God that Alfaro Diaz was *my* father!'

Emma stared at him unhappily. 'You don't — not really.'

'What do you mean?' He swung round.

'Miguel, no matter how you may rile against it, you're Carlos Salvaje's son, and were you not, you wouldn't be the man you are — can't you see that? You're a very lucky man — you have a talent envied by millions, you have the power to induce magic from an instrument made of wood and metal! That's no small achievement. Don't belittle it by resentment. Whatever — your father is like, whatever his faults, he loves you, make no mistake about that. And that's why he took me to see your mother this morning — because he wanted to hurt you, as you've hurt him by marrying me!'

'*I? Hurt him?*' Miguel laughed contemptuously. 'I haven't hurt him! I've thwarted him, that's all.'

'All right, have it your way. But whichever it is, you're not winning any victories by hiding away here, attempting to destroy the one thing in the world you really care about — your music!'

Emma trembled at the violence in his face. 'How do you

know what I care about? Why should you imagine my triumph as a concert pianist is due to anything more inspiring than a craving on my father's part for a vicarious success?'

'I believe it because no one – no *other* person – could inspire such dedication, such attention to detail, such emotive perfection! That's why you're successful, Miguel. Not because someone else is driving you on, but because you play with your mind as well as body. People can sense this; it's that indefinable quality that no amount of cultivation can ever simulate. It's something that's there – in you. It's been there since you were born.' She stared desperately at him. 'Can't you see? Can't you understand? Don't you know how lucky you are to have a gift like that?' She made a sweeping gesture encompassing the magnificent room. 'I've no doubt there are pianists all over the world without the facilities or the opportunities to make use of their talent, but you're not one of them. You have all this – everything that anyone could desire – yet you still pretend that your father is only doing it for himself, for some selfish idea of gaining prestige! What need has he of such things? Don't you think what he already has achieved is enough?'

Miguel moved his shoulders in a defeated gesture. 'You don't understand,' he said heavily. 'I never wanted to be a – a performer! I liked to play, yes. I had an aptitude for the piano, yes. But when my father recognized this he employed the most expensive tutors he could find.' He shrugged. 'I didn't object. Why should I? I loved music. I wanted to learn everything there was to know.' He ran his fingers lovingly over the smooth polished surface of the piano. 'I played everything. Not just classical, but all kinds of music. I used to spend hours, just entertaining myself. I think even then it was an escape.' His features hardened. 'But then my father intervened – his favourite pastime, as you will discover.' His lips were bitter. 'He told me I was wasting my

155

time, wasting all the training he had paid so highly for. He said I should give up composing—' He halted abruptly. 'I should explain. In those days I used to compose quite a lot. Nothing great, you understand, but little pieces that pleased me. I used to imagine that one day I might write something really remarkable – a symphony, or a concerto perhaps.' He sighed. 'That was what I really wanted. I had no desire to become famous as a performer, to play before thousands of people—'

'And yet you do it so – so naturally!' she breathed.

Miguel dropped down on to the piano-stool and touched the keys softly. 'That is because I pretend,' he said, looking up at her, the anger disappearing from his face. 'I pretend I am here – alone – and when it is over I am almost shocked to hear the applause.' He half smiled. 'An admission indeed from someone reputed to be so calm on the platform. But I gain nothing from an audience, they do not lift me, as they say. I am always glad when it is over.'

Emma digested this slowly. She recalled the first time he had come to her father's house in London, the way he had pleaded with her to have dinner with him, how he had wanted to avoid recognition. She had thought he was ashamed of being seen with her, but she could have been wrong. For the first time she felt close to her husband, as though by the admission of his vulnerability he had opened a door and let her see through.

'*Bravo! Bravo!*' The sardonic voice was like a douche of cold water, and the opening door slammed abruptly. Carlos Salvaje walked into the room, and everything was as it was before. His presence had destroyed the gentle intimacy which had been developing between them, and Miguel's face as he faced his father was cool and emotionless.

'What a clever girl, you are, Emma,' Carlos went on smoothly, ignoring the tenseness of her expression. 'I am afraid I underestimated you. When you said you could do it,

I didn't believe you!'

'I didn't – that is–' Emma stared at Carlos disbelievingly, and then glanced imploringly at her husband's face. 'Miguel, I didn't say that—'

Miguel rose to his feet. 'Whether you did or did not is not of the least importance to me,' he replied, but although his tone was cool it would have taken a mind reader to know whether or not he was angry with her.

Carlos looked at him impatiently. 'Do I take it the vigil is over?' he asked, controlling his annoyance with obvious difficulty.

Miguel shrugged. 'How dramatic you make it sound, *padre*. If my seeking a little solitude is regarded as a vigil, then yes, I suppose you could say it is over.' He moved away from the piano and pulling a cord the long jade curtains were swept back to admit the brilliance of the afternoon sun.

Carlos turned his attention to Emma. 'And what has my son been telling you to make you look so drawn, little one?' He flicked a careless hand towards her pale cheeks, but Emma flinched away from him and he smiled derisively. 'So? You are angry with me, too? Because I teased you.' His eyes narrowed. 'Or has this been the time for confessions – for weeping on the shoulder?'

Miguel swung round irritably. 'Why have you come here, *padre*? Are there no distractions on the terrace? Are the other members of this little house party poor entertainment?'

Carlos's lips tightened. 'I should have thought you were better equipped to answer that than I!'

'What is that supposed to mean?' Miguel glared at him, and Emma moved uncomfortably, wishing herself far from this confrontation. She was the outsider here, the unwanted third, and she half believed they had forgotten she was there.

157

Carlos folded his arms. 'You know perfectly well what I mean, Miguel. Do not pretend my wishes concerning you and Carmen were wholly the result of an overcharged imagination!'

Emma caught her breath, and the small sound that escaped her reached Miguel's ears. His lips twisted and he deliberately reached for her, dragging her close against him, within the circle of his arm.

'How unfortunate, *padre*,' he said mockingly. 'For once, I have to disappoint you. But Emma and I are very happy, as you can see, and when our son is born I am convinced you will take to the role of *abuelo* like the flamingo to the lake!'

Abuelo! Emma knew that word. It meant *grandfather*! She wriggled protestingly in her husband's grasp, but although to outward appearances he was looking tenderly down at her, the steel in his eyes brooked no argument.

Carlos stared at his son incredulously. 'You cannot mean—'

'But yes, *padre*, that is what I am saying.' He put his hand lightly but possessively on Emma's middle. 'Emma is *encinta;* we are going to have a child!'

'But how can this be? You have only been married a week!' Carlos's scepticism was tinged with anxiety.

'How *pasado de moda* you are, *padre*. How old-fashioned! Emma is a modern young woman, not a *duena*-escorted *doncella*! We have been lovers since the beginning.'

The sun went down on that day in a blaze of glory, but Emma paid little attention to it. For the past couple of hours she had been lying on her bed staring unseeingly at the ceiling. She dreaded the moment when she would have to leave this sanctuary and join the others for dinner, particularly as she was sure that Carlos would waste no time in telling everyone of her condition.

Of Miguel, she had seen nothing since she left him in the music room after his shattering announcement. She didn't know what Carlos said after she left, she had only known that she could not stand there and listen to a discussion about a fictitious pregnancy that had only been conceived in Miguel's mind.

She buried her face in the pillow, but tears would not come. What a terrible mess! She loved a man who had married her solely to prove to his father that he had a mind and a will of his own . . .

Eventually she stirred, and after a shower dressed in one of her new gowns, a long, amber-coloured chiffon, that swathed the warm contours of her body, and hinted at the curves beneath. Surveying herself in the mirror before leaving her room, she knew she had never looked more attractive, the hollows of anxiety giving her face a haunted beauty.

Juan was alone in the lounge when she appeared and he gave her an admiring smile. 'Marvellous!' he exclaimed. 'You look—' He kissed his fingers extravagantly.

Emma managed a smile. 'Could I have a drink, please?'

'But of course. What will you have? Cinzano? Sherry? Or something a little stronger?'

'Something a little stronger, please.' Emma moved to the long windows which opened on to the terrace. It was dark outside, but the fragrance of the garden was still in the air. She breathed deeply, calming herself, and then turned to accept the gin and vermouth Juan offered.

Juan stood beside her, holding a glass of tequila rather absently, studying her averted face. 'Something is wrong,' he said. 'Do you want to talk about it?'

Emma sighed, tracing the rim of her glass with her forefinger. 'I met Miguel's mother today.'

'I know you did.' Juan frowned. 'It has upset you?'

'Not in the way I think you mean.' She looked up, her eyes wide and distressed. 'Oh, why do Miguel and his father seem to hate one another?'

'They don't hate one another.' Juan shook his head. 'Emma, I know this is hard for you to understand, but it is because they are so much alike that Carlos and Miguel are constantly in conflict. Unfortunately, I feel, Miguel feels a strong sense of loyalty towards his mother, and it is this that from time to time erupts into violence in his relationships.'

'Unfortunately?' Emma was confused. 'Why should it be unfortunate that Miguel feels loyalty towards his mother? Surely it's the most natural thing in the world?'

Juan sighed. 'As I say, it is difficult for you to understand, Emma. Our customs are not your customs, and what happened thirty-three years ago should not be allowed to destroy the present. Carlos is a possessive man so far as Miguel is concerned, you must know this is true, and he resents any attempt on Miguel's part to thwart that possessiveness.' He studied the liquid in his glass thoughtfully. 'Perhaps he hoped that Miguel would never learn the truth of his parentage, but Elissa saw to it that he did.'

'Elissa?' Emma frowned now. 'Who is Elissa?'

'Elissa was Don Carlos's wife. She died almost twenty-five years ago.'

'Oh, yes. He told me his wife was dead.'

'That is correct. She was not well for many years. She became mean and embittered.' He swallowed a little of his tequila. 'Not that I am excusing what happened. No one could do that. But you have no doubt gathered, even in this short time, that what Don Carlos wants he invariably gets, and in this instance it was a son.'

'You mean – Miguel's father took – took Maria as his mistress?'

'Yes.' Juan was obviously finding it difficult to go on, but he persevered. 'Maria was already of a marriageable age. She was sixteen, and here one marries so much younger. Her family were farmers, not rich, you understand, but not peasants either. They were of poor Spanish descent, and very proud. Alfaro was working for Don Carlos at this time. He is what is called a *mestizo*, that is a person of mixed Spanish and Indian blood. After – after Don Carlos's son was born, he persuaded her parents to allow Maria to marry Alfaro. He gave them money and a house, on the understanding that none of this should ever come out. The child was to be brought up as Don Carlos's son, he was legally adopted, and although Elissa had obviously hated the whole affair, she made no immediate objections.' Juan shrugged. 'Perhaps the baby, small and defenceless, was not something to hate. Only as Miguel began to grow, as he developed his father's characteristics, did Elissa turn against him. When he was seven, she told him who his mother really was.' He swallowed the remainder of his drink in a gulp. 'I do not think Miguel has ever really got over it.'

'I see.' Emma realized she had not touched her drink and raised the glass automatically to her lips. 'And Don Carlos?'

'He was furious, as you can imagine, but Elissa died soon afterwards and so escaped his wrath.'

'And I suppose Miguel wanted to spend time with his mother – with his half-brothers and sisters?'

Juan nodded. 'Of course. Knowing Miguel as you do, you must know he is not a man to avoid problems simply because it is easier to do so. Don Carlos objected, of course, but what could he do, short of beating the boy? And he *loved* him, that was the most important thing.' He made an involuntary gesture. 'Perhaps he loves him too much.'

The sound of footsteps in the hall precluded any further discussion and Juan moved away towards the centre of the floor as Carmen Silveiro came into the room. Tonight the

Spanish girl was wearing black, and the smooth flesh of her throat rising from the low-cut bodice had the creamy thickness of magnolia petals. She really was quite startlingly beautiful and Emma felt her throat tighten in despair. How could she ever have hoped to challenge a woman like this? A woman confident and sophisticated and overwhelmingly sure of herself and of her position in this household? And what other reason could Miguel have for rejecting her except an insane desire to oppose his father?

Carmen glanced indifferently at Emma, assessing her and dismissing her, and then looked at Juan. 'Where is Miguel this evening?' she inquired mockingly. 'Surely as he ate no lunch, he must need food! Or has *love*—' the word was a sneer, '—destroyed his appetite?'

'Miguel is dining out this evening,' observed Carlos, entering the room behind her, suave and handsome in his evening clothes. His gaze flickered to Emma, and she felt peculiarly like a fly on a pin. 'I am afraid we are all to be deprived of his company, even Emma.' He smiled thinly, and Emma felt tense. Now it would come, now he would tell them what Miguel had said, and how was she to answer them?

But she was wrong. Carlos turned instead to Juan, making some comment about the estate, and the moment passed. Nevertheless, throughout that long evening she waited with bated breath for him to reveal what he knew, and she wondered whether in fact she was underestimating him. How easy it would be to snap the tension; she could do it herself, but he knew she wouldn't, and how much more enjoyable it was for him to sit back and watch her as she waited for his move, knowing that her nerves were being stretched to screaming point . . .

CHAPTER ELEVEN

THE following morning, after breakfast had been brought to her room again, Emma bathed and dressed and then walked along the tiled passage to the wide hall. Sunlight bathed everything in a golden glow, striking sparks of fire from the polished metal of the Indian lamps. Instead of entering the lounge, she turned through the opened doors on to the terrace and stood looking at the view without any of the anticipation she had felt the day before.

Suddenly the unexpected sound of the helicopter broke the stillness, sending the brightly plumaged macaws shrieking into the air, and as she watched the helicopter itself rose above a belt of trees, hovering like some huge bird before flying off towards the blue line of the mountains.

Emma frowned. Since their arrival two nights ago, the helicopter had been stored in a huge hangar near the stables and there had been no talk last evening of anyone leaving today.

Shrugging, she turned to walk back into the house, and as she did so Carlos appeared. Immediately, Emma stiffened. If he was about to ask her to go riding with him again, he was going to be disappointed.

'*Buenos dias,* Emma,' he remarked, pleasantly enough, but his smile, she thought, had a predatory quality about it.

'Good morning.' Emma was brief, and would have continued on her way had not Carlos gone on:

'You have been watching Miguel leave?'

She halted uncertainly, and looked back at him. 'What did you say?'

'I said – have you been watching Miguel leave in the

163

helicopter?' Carlos looked innocent, but she knew his question was not.

Taking a step back towards him, her hands thrust deep into the pockets of the denim jeans she was wearing, she said: 'Are you trying to tell me something, *señor*?'

'Oh! *Señor*! So formal!' Carlos shook his head. 'My dear, I am your father-in-law, as Miguel says – soon to be the grandfather of your child. Surely you can permit yourself to call me Carlos.'

Emma seethed with impatience. 'What do you mean by saying that Miguel has gone away?'

'Carlos!'

'All right – Carlos!' Emma gritted her teeth.

'That is better.' He smiled again. 'We should not be so formal with one another.'

'Will you please go on – Carlos?'

He sighed. 'Very well. Miguel has gone away. What could be more simple than that? You mean he didn't tell you?'

'You must know he didn't.' Emma felt tremulous, but she refused to let him see it. 'Where – where has he gone?'

'Carlos!'

'All right. Where has he gone, Carlos?' She wanted to scream with frustration.

Carlos stroked his chin thoughtfully. 'I do not know whether I should tell you. After all, Miguel may have withheld this information on purpose. It may be that he does not wish you to know. After yesterday, I am loath to interfere.'

Emma didn't believe him. She didn't believe a word he was saying. He was merely playing with her, and her most sensible course of action would be to leave him alone to tell her in his own good time. If he thought she was interested he was likely to keep her dangling like a fish panting on a hook. Oh, yes, she thought, Miguel might well have justification for his bitterness and frustration. Right now, her strongest desire was to slap that mocking smile from his face.

Gathering her small store of composure, she managed to remain calm. 'Well, if you really feel I shouldn't be told, then I can't force you,' she said. 'Excuse me. I was about to go to my room.'

Carlos regarded her intently, and there was a trace of irritability in his eyes. 'You think you are so clever, don't you?' he said. 'Tricking my son into marrying you by the oldest method in the world!'

Emma's eyes widened. Did this mean that Carlos believed Miguel's story of her pregnancy? Did he imagine that their marriage had been her idea? Or was this merely a way of salving his own conscience? Of assuring himself that Miguel would never have gone against his wishes without good cause?

Shaking her head, she moved to leave him, but his hand curved round her upper arm. Emma shook him off, but his eyes stayed her. 'You are not legally married yet, *señorita*,' he said, and there was no mockery in his tones now. 'A civil ceremony performed in a British register office means nothing in the eyes of my church. You are a fool if you think you can call yourself a Salvaje before you have been married before the priest in the cathedral at Puebla!'

Emma dragged herself away. She was trembling all over and she knew that unless she left him quickly she would disgrace herself by bursting into tears in front of him.

But in her room, the tears would not come. Instead, she sat dry-eyed before her mirror, wishing she had never taken the trouble to visit her godfather on his birthday.

No one seemed to know where Miguel had gone and why. If his father knew he was not telling, while the others were as ignorant of his motives as Emma herself.

The days passed slowly. With time on her hands, Emma spent more and more of it at the stables, talking in halting

Spanish to José, the groom, and helping him exercise the horses. There were three mares and four stallions, and José explained that Don Carlos bred horses for the bullring. It was a profitable sideline and one which Don Carlos could take an active interest in himself.

Loren seemed to find plenty to do about the house. Don Carlos apparently appreciated her services in clearing up his own correspondence and consequently she was not around to keep Emma company.

Juan, too, had work of his own to occupy him, but occasionally he walked in the grounds with Emma and once they took a rowing boat out on the lake.

The surroundings were so magnificent that she should have been happy, but she wasn't. She ached for news of Miguel, and from time to time she felt a deep resentment that he should think he could bring her here and then just abandon her. Where was he? Who was he with? And when would he return?

In one respect at least, Don Carlos had not run true to form, she thought. He had told no one of her supposed pregnancy, and she wondered why. The only solution she could come up with was that by not mentioning it he could pretend it wasn't there. And it wasn't, a hysterical voice inside her cried. How could it be when their marriage was no marriage at all?

Once Juan took her driving in a Landrover that Don Carlos used in wet weather for getting about the estate. Until then she had imagined that the only means of access to this mountainous area was by the use of the helicopter, but now she discovered there was a road, such as it was.

A mountainous track, pitted with potholes, wound through a dried-up gully, and it was possible to reach Puebla in a matter of hours. The route in miles was not distant, but the conditions were such that one had to drive very carefully.

Juan stopped the Landrover at the head of the pass and Emma looked down on the estate spread out below her. It was early morning, and the lake was lemon-tinged, its edges darkening to purplish green. The reflection of the mountains cast their shadows like giants crouched at bay, and she marvelled that anyone could have created such beauty and cultivation from what must have been wild and savage countryside.

Now she looked at Juan and said: 'When do you think Miguel will come back? Don't you really know where he has gone?'

Juan looked as though he had been expecting these questions, but he could only shake his head. 'I do not know anything,' he answered honestly. 'I cannot understand why he found it necessary to go alone.'

Emma realized that Juan was hurt by this aspect of the affair. 'But surely Don Carlos must know something. Where is the helicopter? Why doesn't he try to have it located if he is worried?'

'I have no doubt that the helicopter is at the airfield in Puebla. You remember – where you met Felipe Alvarez?'

'You think Miguel is in Puebla?' Her heart leapt.

'No. But the helicopter will wait there.'

'And if Don Carlos needs it in the meantime?'

'Don Carlos rarely leaves the estate. But if he should require to do so, he has only to send a message.'

'Of course.' Emma sighed. 'I don't know what to think!'

Juan shrugged. 'I shouldn't think Miguel would confide in his father at this time.'

'Perhaps you're right.' Emma was doubtful. 'Oh, Juan, I wish he would come back!' Her lips trembled and he gave an exasperated ejaculation. Covering both her hands with one of his, he said softly:

'You're in love with Miguel! I never realized . . .'

Emma could not reply. She was too distressed, and to her relief Juan sensed this and said no more, but started the engine and began the drive back to the house.

Occasionally she was tempted to go and visit Maria Diaz, but she was afraid that if she did so, Carlos would distort what she had done when he accounted her movements to Miguel.

One evening, about ten days after Miguel had left, Emma entered the lounge before dinner to find only Carmen Silveiro in occupation. She was surprised, because normally this was the time of day she liked best, when she and Juan shared a drink together before the meal and before anyone else arrived. Carmen was usually last to appear, and this made it doubly surprising.

'Do sit down,' she said, throwing a languid hand towards the soft hide couch, but Emma chose a chair. 'What will you drink?'

'Er – just sherry, please.' Emma spread her skirts. She was quite content to let Carmen behave as though she was the hostess here. In that respect she had no aspirations whatsoever, whereas it was obvious that Carmen coveted her role.

The Mexican girl handed her the glass and Emma took it, holding it lightly between her fingers. Carmen, she noticed, took nothing, but came to stand before her, looking down on her with rather discomfiting intensity.

Emma glanced round. Where was Juan? Why didn't he come? She had no desire to enter into a *tête-à-tête* with the woman Carlos had expected Miguel to marry.

'Tell me, *señorita*,' Carmen began, examining the long painted nails that extended from her fingers, 'when is it going to become apparent to you that so long as you are here Miguel will not come back?'

Her words, spoken so calmly and so quietly, were far more shocking than a violent ejaculation would have been.

They caused Emma's whole body to film with sweat and her initial reaction was to get up out of the chair and leave the room. But then common sense prevailed, and she realized that to do so would merely give the other girl a small victory. So, sipping her sherry, she pretended a calmness she did not feel.

Carmen's nostrils flared. 'Did you hear what I said?'

Emma looked up. 'Yes, I heard. However, I don't happen to believe you. I've no doubt that – that Carlos put you up to this, and I am quite used to his – little eccentricities.'

The Mexican girl looked furious. 'How dare you speak to me like that?'

'How dare I?' Emma felt amazingly cool now. 'Surely, as Miguel's wife, I have more right here than you have.'

'I live here!' said Carmen arrogantly. 'This is my home.'

Emma shrugged. 'And for the moment, it's mine, too.'

'Never!' Carmen was adamant. She walked restlessly about the room. 'Why do you think Miguel has gone away?'

Now Emma pretended an interest in her drink. She could not let Carmen read the uncertainty in her eyes which appeared whenever she seriously tried to find an answer to that. 'Do you know why he has gone away?' she asked.

Carmen plucked impatiently at the material of her gown. 'I know he has gone to Mexico City,' she said, and then as though realizing she was answering questions instead of just asking them, she went on: 'But if you are truly his wife, if he really intends to come back, he would have told you that.'

'If he had told me,' said Emma carefully, 'why should you imagine I would tell you?'

Carmen sneered, 'Oh, please, do not pretend with me! You did not even know he was leaving, let alone where he was going. And the purpose behind his trip is a mystery to us all. Although I think Carlos knows something – but he is not telling. They are very close, those two.'

'You think so?' Emma was sardonic.

'But of course. Oh, do not think this little upset over your arrival will last for long. You are not used to us, *señorita*, you do not understand the Latin temperament. Miguel will come back and all will be forgiven, you will see. But as for you—' She snapped her fingers. 'I do not give that for your chances!'

'That will do, Carmen!' As before Carlos silenced his niece, entering the room with a cat-like noiseless tread that could unnerve Emma on occasion. He looked down at her, still seated in her chair, and raised his eyebrows. 'This will not do. Two beautiful women quarrelling over my son. I am jealous!'

But he was mocking her and Emma knew it. Getting to her feet, praying her legs would support her, she said, as casually as she could:

'Where is Juan?'

Carlos moved his broad shoulders indolently. 'You do not know?'

'Oh, stop this cat-and-mouse game!' Emma was becoming distraught, but although Carlos answered her civilly enough, she sensed his pleasure in her distress.

'Juan has gone to see Miguel. He left this afternoon. José drove him to the railway station at Vasos, and from there he will take a train to Mexico City.'

Emma was aghast. 'You mean – there has been word from Miguel? Why wasn't I informed?'

Carlos shrugged. 'The message was not for you. It was for Juan, as I have said.'

'But why didn't Juan tell me he was going to see Miguel?' Emma was really distressed now.

Carlos spread his hands. 'That is not my affair.' He glanced knowingly at Carmen. 'It would seem, Emma, that so far as Miguel is concerned you have ceased to exist.'

'*No!*' The word was torn from her. 'No, I don't believe you.'

Carlos grimaced. 'That is up to you, of course.'

'How do I know you're not just making this up?'

'Find Loren – ask her. She must know that Juan left this afternoon.'

Emma drew a trembling breath. Facing the two of them, she felt totally inadequate, totally unable to cope. With a muffled sob, she turned and fled out of the room and down the hall until she reached her bedroom. Once there she slammed shut the door and flung herself on her bed, and now the tears did come, hot, choking sobs that tore up through her body, shredding her emotions, devastating her . . .

No one came to find her, and she didn't expect them to. No one cared about her in this house, and now that Juan was gone she felt as though her only friend had deserted her. He might have told her he was leaving, but then so might Miguel, and with more reason. She would never begin to understand either of them.

A sense of despair, of homesickness, gripped her. How far away her life in London seemed, not just in miles, but in experience. These last few days she seemed to have run through the whole gamut of her emotions and there was nothing left; she felt completely drained.

This marriage was a farce, perpetrated in anger, and without any basis on which to build. If Miguel had stayed, if they had tried to make something out of the vague attraction he sometimes felt for her, perhaps it would have been different. But then she had only herself to blame that their marriage had not been consummated. That night in this very room, he had *wanted* her, she had known that, but she, fool that she was, had thought she could wait until there was more than just wanting. And now he was gone, and whether or not he intended to return made little difference. Their relationship had never seemed more remote.

Some words of Tennyson's filtered through her brain: *we die, does it matter when?* They were appropriate somehow, only in this case it was the death of a marriage. Did it matter when it was over? Sooner or later it was bound to happen, and could she bear it if the victory was Carlos's after all? Did she want to stay here for more humiliation, more contempt? Was she prepared to give Carmen the satisfaction of seeing her treated by her husband as she had been treated by his father? *No!*

She sat bolt upright on the bed. She refused to contemplate such a thing. She might not have much to commend her, but she had her pride, and so long as she remained here she was inviting contempt.

She slid off the bed and walked to the long windows looking out on the moon-painted landscape. It was all beautiful. She had never seen anything so beautiful. It appealed to the sensitivity of her nature. But like all gardens of Eden, there had to be a serpent; in this case two.

So what was she to do? She could go to Mexico City and try to find Miguel and ask him what his intentions were, but that seemed totally ineffectual. How on earth did one go about trying to trace someone in a foreign city when apart from everything else one did not even speak the language? She could go to Puebla and question the pilot of the helicopter, but that sounded unlikely. And in any case why should she assume he would tell her anything without first gaining Carlos's approval?

So what was she left with? Only two alternatives. To stay here – or go home!

Home!

What a delightful sound that word had, and what reassuring associations. Mrs. Cook was looking after the house until her father returned. She would be glad to see Emma. Oh, how marvellous it would be to feel wanted and sheltered and protected again!

She turned and surveyed the room behind her. She could leave in the morning. No one was likely to try and stop her. On the contrary, she was almost prepared to believe this whole series of incidents was a carefully designed plot to achieve just this end.

All the same, the idea of facing Carlos and telling him she was leaving did not appeal to her. She could almost see the look of delighted anticipation in his eyes, hear him consoling her with platitudes when all the while he was secretly laughing at her.

No, somehow she couldn't face that. She would have to leave without his knowledge. She could send him a cablegram from Mexico City a few minutes before her flight took off, so that if for some nefarious reason of his own he found it unacceptable to have her leave at this time, he would not be able to stop her.

It was amazing how once one's mind was made up, things could run in such a way as to make her plans almost easy to accomplish. As Juan had taken her driving in the Landrover, it was not a particularly difficult feat to suggest to Carlos after breakfast next morning that she might use the vehicle herself.

Carlos seemed morose, occupied with his own thoughts, and made no demur, so that ten o'clock found Emma on her way up the mountainous track towards the dried-up gully pass. Of course, she had not been able to bring much with her without causing comment, just a large vanity case into which she had stuffed a couple of changes of underwear, a dress and some trousers, but fortunately her old clothes would be still in her wardrobe in London as she didn't think Mrs. Cook was likely to have thrown them out without her father's permission.

Her greatest anxiety had been in obtaining her passport from Miguel's room. She had never entered his bedroom before, and there had been a painful delight in doing so. It was a much plainer room than hers, with a polished floor strewn with rugs, and dark blue bedcovers and curtains. She had not even been certain she would find her passport there, but a swift check through his bureau had produced not only her passport but his.

She had looked at his picture for a long time. The fact that his passport was there proved that he intended to come back at some time and also that he had not left the country. For a moment, her determination had faltered, but then she had told herself that even if he did come back things would never be the same, so she might as well break with him now before something irreparable happened. Like a child, she thought, biting her lips to stop them from trembling.

The journey to Puebla was the most uncomfortable journey she had ever made. Apart from the discomfort of the deplorable road conditions, she was also gripped with a nervous anticipation that Carlos would not let her get away with this, and any minute she expected to hear the helicopter overhead, on its way to Lacustre Largo.

But, in fact, nothing happened, and her only feeling was one of intense tiredness and emptiness when she reached Puebla.

It was the middle of the afternoon by this time, and she asked a policeman in halting Spanish where the railway station might be. But he merely shook his head, explaining volubly, half of which Emma did not understand, that there was no railway station, and the only way she could reach Mexico City was by coach.

But the coach depot proved just as unhelpful. There were no buses leaving for Mexico City until the following morning, and she dared not wait that long. Her only means of escape was the Landrover, and while she supposed Carlos could accuse her of stealing it even that was preferable to waiting here for him to send someone to pick her up.

She bought some petrol and managed to obtain some coffee from a vending machine. It tasted good, so as she was hungry she bought some fruit and a round loaf of corn bread. Then she got her bearings and with a sense of trepidation set off to drive to Mexico City. It was less than a hundred miles away, she knew, and yet she also knew that with her limited experience of driving on these roads it could take several hours.

But what she had really not been prepared for was the absolute darkness which fell soon after she left Puebla. Her abortive attempt to find a railway station, having her coffee and buying the petrol, not to mention the fruit and bread, had all taken time and night fell with an eerie suddenness on a bleak and unfriendly landscape. The moon which had been so bright the night before at Lacustre Largo had obviously spent itself, and she thought it was just her luck to pick such a night to travel so far.

There was little traffic on the road, and sometimes she went several miles without meeting anything, which wasn't encouraging, but she pressed on, telling herself that it would not take much longer, and boosting her morale with thoughts of London, the house in Kensington, and Mrs. Cook . . .

She reached the outskirts of her destination soon after nine and drove straight to the airport. But of course, there were no flights leaving that night and the earliest they could accommodate her was the following morning.

She made a booking and then had to think about accommodation. She daren't stay in the airport hotel in case Carlos tried to trace her there, so she found a small *pension* that was not too far away and after being shown her room decided to go straight to bed.

But not to sleep. For all she was so weary she couldn't rest, and she spent the night prowling about her bedroom, alternately longing and dreading the day that was to come.

At last fingers of light crept up the sky and she was able to dress and leave the hotel without causing too much speculation. She drove to the airport, and parked the Landrover in what she hoped was a safe area. Someone would be bound to find it there, she thought.

The international airport was air-conditioned and impersonal, thronged with people coming and going from various parts of the world. In her cotton trousers and a sleeveless sweater, a light jacket over her arm, she looked like a student, and attracted no more attention in spite of her lack of luggage. These days, standards had changed, and she was glad to feel anonymous.

The reception desks were busy with people checking and collecting their reservations. Emma joined the queue resignedly. She had no hurry. Her flight did not leave for more than two hours.

But even as she slipped into her place, a man who had been standing with his back to her at one side of the desk turned, and she found herself looking at Miguel.

CHAPTER TWELVE

THE colour drained out of Emma's cheeks and she thought she would have fallen had he not moved swiftly and grasped her arm, drawing her gently but irrevocably aside, his fingers hard and cool on her arm.

'*Dios*, Emma!' he muttered fiercely. 'What are you trying to do to me?'

Only then did Emma gather enough strength to look up at him and saw the lines of fatigue and strain in his face. 'I – I – don't know what you mean,' she faltered. 'Wh-what are you doing here? Are – are you leaving Mexico too?'

'*Cristo*, Emma, do not be foolish! I am here because of you – to find *you*!'

He glanced round impatiently, aware of the gathering tide of interest engendered by the passengers waiting at the reception desks. Urging her forward, ignoring the protest she would have made, he propelled her towards the exit, saying: 'We cannot talk here. I have a car outside.'

Emma struggled vigorously. 'I can't go with you! I – my booking – the plane leaves in a short time. I have to confirm my booking!'

Miguel's face was grim. 'There is no booking. I have cancelled it,' he replied shortly.

'No – no booking? What do you mean? You can't have cancelled it!'

'But I have. You forget, Emma, you are my wife. You will not be going anywhere without my permission.'

Emma's heart pounded heavily, and she stared at him with a feeling mingled of despair and frustration. How had he known she might be at the airport? Who could have told him? And why was he forcing her to stay when he so obviously didn't want her?

'How – how did you know where to find me?' she demanded jerkily, but he did not reply. They were crossing the parking area, his long strides forcing her to run a little to keep up with him.

Retaining his hold on her arm, he stopped beside a sleek grey limousine and unlocking the door he opened it and thrust her inside. He slid in after her and she had to move quickly across the seat to avoid being crushed.

'Miguel, please—' she began, but he just shook his head wordlessly and pulled her closely into his arms, burying his face in the softness of her nape.

'Emma! Ema!' he groaned, and she could feel he was trembling. 'Don't ever try to run away from me again.'

Emma was confused. This was not the Miguel who had gone so recklessly after what he had wanted in London, and nor was he the Miguel who had become so cold and remote after their marriage. This man was holding her as if he could not bear to ever let her go, and when he lifted his head to seek her mouth with his, there was a desperate hunger in his kiss.

But Emma resisted him. Her nerves were torn and shredded, but she still refused to submit. She would not allow him to think he could leave her alone with his father and Carmen at Lacustre Largo for almost two weeks without sending her any word whatsoever, and then assume that he could simply take her in his arms and by his undoubted expertise induce her trembling obedience.

Miguel sensed her withdrawal immediately, and lifted his head, looking down into her eyes so intently that she had to look away from him. 'So?' he said softly, 'you are not pleased to see me!'

Emma took a breath. 'How – how can *you* say that? I've been waiting to see you for eleven days!' Her voice broke a little at the end, but she tried to disguise it, and his lips curved rather wryly.

'So many days!' he said. 'You were counting them?'

Emma felt the hot colour burn in her cheeks. 'Don't try to make a fool of me!' she cried tremulously, and then stared concentratedly out of the window, willing the hot tears that were burning behind her eyes not to fall.

Miguel lifted a hand to stroke her cheek, but she flinched away from his touch, and as she did so she saw that the bandages had gone from his injured hand, and in their place were bands of adhesive tape, individually supporting each finger.

Miguel shrugged, and allowed his hand to fall. 'I am sorry,' he said softly. 'I did not mean to tease you.'

Emma endeavoured to calm herself. 'What do you intend to do with me? Am I to be allowed to take my flight?'

'*No!*' At that, Miguel's voice hardened and for a moment she glimpsed the steel beneath his velvet touch. He rested his head back against the soft upholstery and looking up at the roof of the car, said: 'Juan told me you loved me!'

'*Wh-what?*' Emma was first incredulous, and then hotly humiliated, indignant and disappointed with Juan that he should betray her confidence in such a way. Clenching her fists, she glanced towards Miguel. 'I see,' she said, controlling her voice with difficulty. 'Is that why you're here? I can assure you there's absolutely no need for you to feel any kind of responsibility for me! I want nothing more to do with this family, and as soon as I get back to England I intend to have the marriage annulled. I'm quite prepared to have a medical test, if necessary—'

Miguel turned back to her, supporting his head on his fist, his arm resting on the back of the seat. 'Be still!' he said, and although he spoke quietly there was a wealth of command in the two words. Studying her flushed cheeks and trembling body, he half smiled. 'What a lot of nonsense you can talk when you are afraid to face the truth!'

179

'I'm not afraid to face the truth!' she declared fiercely, 'and I should tell you, in my country just because a person is married to someone it doesn't mean that they hold the power of life and death over them!'

'There you go again,' he said, and she bent her head in miserable embarrassment. 'Now,' he went on, 'let me say something. You are my wife, and my wife you are going to stay. Let me make that clear right from the beginning, and there will be no annulment, because by tomorrow no court in the world would grant you one. Do I make myself clear?'

Emma stared at him uneasily, her breath coming swiftly. 'I don't know what you mean.'

'Oh, yes, you do.' He tugged gently at a strand of amber hair. 'And tonight, or perhaps this afternoon,' his mouth curved sensuously, 'there will be no escape.'

Ideas of escape, of thrusting open the car door and rushing across the airport buildings, and demanding a form of asylum, fled. Her legs would not have supported her, had she tried to do any such thing. But even so, that did not mean that he was going to have his own way.

'So!' He continued to play with her hair as he spoke. 'So, we will have no more talk about aeroplanes and bookings and annulments.'

Emma twisted the strap of her handbag. 'You think you can do what you like with me, don't you? You think that because Juan was foolish enough to tell you something I said once—'

'*Emma!*' One hand closed round her throat, and his eyes were dark and angry now. 'Please! I am asking you. Give me a chance to explain.'

But Emma shook her head, overpoweringly conscious of the strength of those fingers. 'You must think I'm some kind of an idiot,' she exclaimed. 'You go away without telling me where you're going—'

'What is this?' Miguel's brows drew together in a scowl,

and his fingers tightened so cruelly round her throat that she winced.

Immediately he was contrite, relaxing his hold, putting his mouth where the flesh was reddening, deliberately letting his tongue move against her skin so that she had the almost overwhelming urge to lift his mouth to hers.

But the moment passed, and he lifted his head, looking down at her with strange absorption. 'What did you say? You did not get my message?'

'You – know – I didn't,' she murmured unsteadily.

'I do not know any such thing,' he declared distinctly. 'Emma, before God as my witness, I left a message for you with Gomez.'

'Who is Gomez?' she asked faintly.

'A servant. A man I thought I could trust.'

'But why didn't you tell *me*?' she exclaimed.

Miguel sighed. 'The morning I was leaving, I came to your room, but you were sleeping. I did not want to disturb you. Instead, I told Gomez to come and see you when you woke – to tell you that I had to go to Mexico City but that I would be back as soon as I could.'

'I got no message.' Emma's tone was flat, and Miguel's lips twisted.

'No, I realize that now. Oh, Emma, what must you have thought of me?' He smote his uninjured fist against the leather upholstery, but then his eyes narrowed. 'I did not trust the words on paper. I felt sure my father would somehow get his hands on a letter. But obviously I underestimated him.'

'He knew you were leaving?'

'The night before, yes. I went to see my – mother! When I came back, I had to tell him that I intended to use the helicopter the next morning. He asked why, and I said I would rather not say.' He made a helpless gesture. 'Then he said something which – well, which made our conversation less than pleasant.'

'About me, I suppose.'

'I suppose it was.' Miguel chewed his lower lip, scarcely aware of his fingers massaging her shoulder under the ribbed opening of her sweater. But Emma was aware of it, and of the weakness he inspired in her. 'He suggest I should find a clinic here, willing to make certain arrangements regarding your – condition.'

Emma bent her head. Even with her knowledge it was unacceptable. She looked at Miguel compassionately, and when his eyes caught that look, he grasped her hands in both of his, and said: 'Forgive me!'

Emma looked away from him. She did not trust herself to remain unmoved when he put such appeal into his voice. 'Do you know why I didn't get the message, then?'

Miguel sighed. 'I can guess. Emma, Gomez is one of my father's servants, he is regarded by the Indians as their master, the *patrón*. If it came to a showdown, and it must have done, then they would not dare withhold information from him.'

'So that was how he knew you were in Mexico City,' breathed Emma softly.

'He told you that?'

'No, Carmen did. Two nights ago. Your father said he had no idea where you had gone.'

'I might have known he would say that, given the opportunity.' Miguel shook his head. 'And to think, if I hadn't returned home and found you gone, I might have had to travel all the way to England to get you back again.'

Emma drew her fingers from his. 'Why should you want me back?'

'Isn't it obvious?' His voice hardened.

'No, I don't think it is. After all, you only married me to thwart your father—'

'That's not true!' His eyes glittered angrily. 'Who told you that?'

'I didn't need to be told.' Emma moved her shoulders indifferently. 'It was obvious.'

His tone thickened. 'How was it obvious, may I ask?'

Emma quivered. 'Well, of course it was obvious. From the very beginning, you treated me as if I was an unnecessary encumbrance—'

'No!'

'Yes. Why, the night we were married you spent with Juan, working!'

Miguel's eyes narrowed again. 'You mean you would have welcomed me that night?' His eyes probed hers. 'Why, you would not even accept me the night we arrived at my father's house!'

'That – that was different.'

'How was it different?'

'Well, I already was beginning to know you. I knew you didn't really – feel anything!'

'*Madre de Dios! I* did not feel anything?' He smote his forehead with his hand. 'You think I would marry a woman I did not love—'

Emma had heard enough. She put her hands over her ears, and moved her head helplessly from side to side. 'You don't love me! You're only saying you do because of what Juan told you—'

'*No!*' Now Miguel was really angry. Grasping her by the shoulders, wincing as his injured fingers protested at such rough usage, he shook her. 'Why do you think Juan told me that you loved me? Do you think he came right out and said it?'

Emma could only shake her head, and he went on: 'He told me because I was in such a terrible state when I arrived back at Lacustre Largo and found you had disappeared that I think I went a little out of my head!'

Emma stared at him. 'You – saw – Juan? At Lacustre Largo?'

'Of course.'

'But – but he had gone away. To Mexico City! To see you!'

'*Impossible!* Even Juan did not know where to find me.'

Emma's hands dropped. 'But – but your father – he said—'

'Yes? What did he say?' Miguel was impatient, and Emma blinked rapidly, trying to assimilate what she had just heard.

'He – he said they had had word from you. That Juan had gone to see you.' She made a confused gesture. 'And Juan had gone. He wasn't there two days ago.'

Miguel uttered an exclamation. 'I've no doubt he went to see his family at Vasos—'

'*Vasos?* Yes, that was the place your father mentioned. But he said he was going to get a train from there to Mexico City!'

Miguel calmed himself with difficulty. 'Now I begin to see. So he told you that as well as going without leaving you a message, I had sent for Juan, also?'

'Yes.'

'And of course, you could stand no more, so you did exactly what he wanted you to do.'

'I know, I know. I realized that was what he wanted, but – but—'

'But you did not have any confidence.' He allowed his hands to move across her shoulders to cup her neck. 'You did not know, for instance, that I adore you . . .'

Emma made one last attempt to remain aloof. 'But you went away!' she exclaimed. 'Why? Why?'

Miguel bent to touch his mouth to hers, playing with her lips until his own need overcame all else and he crushed her to him. Now Emma did not resist and it was some time before he pressed her away from him, smiling rather wryly.

'I do not intend to seduce my wife in a car park,' he muttered huskily. 'Much as I want you!'

Emma could hardly believe all this was really happening. Was it really less than an hour since she had driven to the airport feeling as though the bottom had dropped out of her world?

'Tell me,' she whispered, 'why did you go away?'

Miguel sighed, and lay back against the soft upholstery. 'I will try to explain. You remember the day after we arrived at my father's house – the day he took you to meet my mother—'

'How could I forget?' Emma was fervent.

'So!' Miguel allowed his fingers to slide along the neckline of her sweater with possessive persistence. 'So you recall that afternoon, in the music room.' She nodded, and he nodded, too. '*Bien,* we seemed close then. And I was content – until my father appeared. Until that afternoon, I was convinced you had married me to protect Harrison—'

'No!' Emma was horrified.

'Why not? We were both adept at hiding our feelings, and you must admit that apart from responding in a purely sexual way, you had never given me any reason to suppose that you found my company desirable.' He shrugged. 'People are strange when they are in love. They do strange things. They have no confidence in themselves. Why should I be any different?'

Emma stretched out her hand and touched his cheek, and he immediately turned her palm to his mouth. 'I will continue,' he murmured gently. 'So – then my father appeared. He was so arrogant, I had to destroy that arrogance. It was crazy, I realize that, but sometimes I do crazy things.'

Emma smiled tremulously. 'I know how you felt,' she averred, recalling her own dealings with Carlos Salvaje.

Miguel spread a hand. 'But, before I go on, I must say that my father is not always so – objectionable. He can be most charming. And when he realizes I mean what I say so far as you are concerned, he will come round, believe me.'

Emma was doubtful, but this was not the time to express doubts. 'Go on about why you went away,' she urged.

'All right. Well, that afternoon I realized that you and I could never make our home with my father. We needed some place of our own, to be alone.' His eyes caressed her and she felt warm all over. 'But my real reason for going away was because of these.' He indicated his fingers. 'When we were in Mexico City, on our way to Lacustre Largo, I saw a specialist. He told me that if I wanted to be able to use my fingers again with as much dexterity, I must have treatment. And that is what I have been having. I needed to be able to support myself and my wife very much; for once I wanted to be independent of my father. I thought perhaps that once we were alone, really alone, I could teach you to love me. I never dreamed . . .' He broke off, and Emma felt a sense of compassion. This side of Miguel's character was so appealing.

'The specialists were not absolutely certain that the cure could be completed when I first visited them,' he went on. 'And I had to know this before I could feel completely free to do as I chose. Can you understand that?'

Emma regarded him sympathetically. 'And?'

'The fingers are healing well. I can play the piano without making too many mistakes.' He smiled. 'But best of all, I have found us a house; it is outside the city, not far from the sea, and that is where we will live from now on.'

Emma tipped her head on one side. 'And when you're on tour?'

'Then you will be with me!' he stated briefly, as though there had never been any doubt about that.

Emma shook her head. 'I can hardly believe it.'

Miguel drew her towards him. 'I'll make you believe it. You've no idea how demanding I can be.' He tangled his fingers in her hair. 'And another thing; a piece of music I wrote – just a small sonata – is to be published!'

'What?' Emma gasped and drew back to look at him. 'How marvellous!'

'Yes, isn't it? I've called it for you.'

Emma felt an enormous wealth of tenderness envelop her. 'Oh, Miguel! I do love you!'

'And I love you,' he replied gravely. 'I've only ever loved two women in all my life. The woman I thought was my mother – and you.'

'Elissa,' said Emma quietly.

'You know about her?' he demanded defensively.

'Yes, Juan told me,' she answered, and his features relaxed.

'I thought my father had been regaling you with all the sordid details,' he muttered.

'They're not sordid,' she protested, kissing his fingers. 'The only pity is that you had to be the innocent victim of her bitterness.'

Miguel shrugged. 'At the time no one can have any idea how I felt. But afterwards, I realized she had had a lot to put up with.'

Emma nodded, and he went on: 'Until then I had been so happy, so secure! I was proud of my heritage.' He shook his head. 'And then Elissa told me the truth, and for a while I hated them both. The only person I couldn't hate was my mother – Maria. But I couldn't love her either. I felt a sense of loyalty towards her and perhaps a little guilt, but never love. I swore when Elissa died I would never marry – never give my affection to any woman ever again.'

'And now?' Emma stared at him.

'Now?' He bent to touch her mouth with his. 'Now, I could not envisage life without you. Now, I will kill any man who tries to take you from me. Does that frighten you?'

'It should,' she admitted honestly. 'But it doesn't. It just makes me feel so – so beloved . . .' And then a thought struck her. 'But what about your father? He still thinks he is going to become a grandfather.'

Miguel laughed softly. 'And isn't he?' he murmured.

Emma flushed then. 'Oh, you know what I mean!'

'Yes, I know.' He looked deeply into her eyes. 'And perhaps for a time he will be disappointed because I want you all to myself. But soon – soon we will satisfy him in that way and then perhaps we will all get some peace, hmm . . .'

Mills & Boon Classics

The very best of Mills & Boon
romances, brought back for those of you
who missed reading them when they
were first published.

There are three other Classics for you to collect this
March

RING OF JADE
by Margaret Way

On the magical tropical island, Brockway's Folly, in the Great
Barrier Reef, Claire met two men — David who needed her
and Adam who didn't. Claire had come to the island to
escape her emotions — but instead she found them threatening
to overwhelm her completely.

THE INSHINE GIRL
by Margery Hilton

Della and Venetia were the best of friends, but the glamorous
Della just couldn't help outshining Venetia all the time. But
was Simon Manville right when he assured Venetia that it was
the 'inshine girls' that most men wanted to marry?

LUCIFER'S ANGEL
by Violet Winspear

When Fay, young and inexperienced, married a sophisticated
film director, and was swept into the brittle, shallow social
whirl of Hollywood, she soon discovered that all too often
there is heartache behind the glitter.

If you have difficulty in obtaining any of these books through
your local paperback retailer, write to:

Mills & Boon Reader Service
P.O. Box 236, Thornton Road, Croydon, Surrey, CR9 3RU.

Mills & Boon Classics

The very best of Mills & Boon
romances, brought back for those of
you who missed reading them
when they were first published.

in
April
we bring back the following four
great romantic titles.

CINDERELLA IN MINK
by Roberta Leigh
Nicola Rosten was used to the flattery and deference accorded
to a very wealthy woman. Yet Barnaby Grayson mistook her
for a down-and-out and set her to work in the kitchen!

MASTER OF SARAMANCA
by Mary Wibberley
Gavin Grant was arrogant and overbearing, thought Jane, and
she hadn't ever disliked anyone quite so much. Yet . . .

NO GENTLE POSSESSION
by Anne Mather
After seven years, Alexis Whitney was returning to Karen's
small town. It was possible that he might not even remember
her — but Karen hoped desperately that he did.

A SONG BEGINS
by Mary Burchell
When Anthea began her training with the celebrated operatic
conductor, Oscar Warrender, she felt her dreams were coming
true — but would she be tough enough to work under such an
exacting taskmaster?

If you have difficulty in obtaining any of these books through
your local paperback retailer, write to:

Mills & Boon Reader Service
P.O. Box 236, Thornton Road, Croydon, Surrey, CR9 3RU.

The Mills & Boon Rose is the Rose of Romance

Every month there are ten new titles to choose from — ten new stories about people falling in love, people you want to read about, people in exciting, far-away places. Choose Mills & Boon. It's your way of relaxing.

March's titles are:

THE MATING SEASON by *Janet Dailey*
When Jonni Starr got engaged, she thought she ought to go back to tell her parents. So back she went, and promptly fell in love with another man . . .

LOVE IS THE HONEY by *Violet Winspear*
Iris agreed that it was time she found out what life was like outside of her convent. So she went to work for the overwhelming Zonar Mavrakis — and found out with a vengeance!

SPIRIT OF ATLANTIS by *Anne Mather*
After the shock of her father's death, Julie was having a restful holiday in Canada. Restful? Not with the disturbing Dan Prescott around!

THE GOLDEN PUMA by *Margaret Way*
The abrasive David Hungerford thought that Catherine ought to leave her father to make a life of her own. But what life was there, without David — who wasn't interested in her in that way?

MAN OF ICE by *Rachel Lindsay*
Happy to accept a job with the kindly Miss Bateman, Abby found that she had brought on herself the contempt and suspicion of her employer's dour nephew Giles Farrow.

HOTEL JACARANDAS by *Katrina Britt*
Julie's sadness over her parents' divorce was nothing compared to her heartbreak when she fell in love with Felipe de Torres y Aquilino — who didn't want her . . .

THE FIRST OFFICER by *Anne Weale*
Four years' separation had not lessened Katy's love for her husband. But Charles had been disillusioned by her once — had she reason to suppose she had any attraction for him now?

NIGHT MUSIC by *Charlotte Lamb*
'I bought you, and what I buy stays bought, even if it proves to be worthless,' Steve Crawford told Lisa. Would she be able to change his opinion of her?

DANGEROUS MARRIAGE by *Mary Wibberley*
Shelley knew nothing about the overbearing and mysterious Vargen Gilev except that she loved him — and he did not love her . . .

YOURS WITH LOVE by *Mary Burchell*
Virginia had fallen in love with Jason Kent as a result of playing 'the other woman' in a plot to get rid of Jason's wife. But how could Virginia go on caring about a man as selfish as he was?

If you have difficulty in obtaining any of these books from your local paperback retailer, write to:

Mills & Boon Reader Service
P.O. Box 236, Thornton Road, Croydon, Surrey CR9 3RU.